That Night

USA TODAY BESTSELLING AUTHOR

K.I. LYNN

That Night
Copyright © K.I. Lynn

ISBN - 978-1-948284-24-0

This book is a work of fiction. Names, characters, places, and incidents either are products of the author's imagination or are used fictitiously. Any resemblance to actual events or locales or persons, living or dead, is entirely coincidental.

This work is copyrighted. All rights are reserved. Apart from any use as permitted under the Copyright Act 1968, no part may be reproduced, copied, scanned, stored in a retrieval system, recorded or transmitted, in any form or by any means, without prior written permission of the author.

Cover image licensed by WANDER AGUIAR : PHOTOGRAPHY
Model: Andrew Biernat
Cover design by Lori Jackson Design

Editor:
Marti Lynch
Nancy Smay
Danielle Leigh

Publication Date: March 23, 2020
Genre: FICTION/Romance/Contemporary
ISBN-13: 978-1948284196
Copyright © 2020 K.I. Lynn
All rights reserved

That Night

SOUNDTRACK

Lykke Li—Little Bit (AutoErotique Bootleg Remix)

8 Letters—Why Don't We

What A Man Gotta Do—Jonas Brothers

Lover—Taylor Swift

Raising Hell—Kesha

Trampoline—SHAED

Someone You Loved—Lewis Capaldi

Unsteady—X Ambassadors

Sucker—Jonas Brothers

365—Katy Perry

Say You Won't Let Go—James Arthur

Lost in the Fire—Gesaffelstein & The Weekend

Electricity—Silk City & Dua Lipa

Almost (Sweet Music)—Hozier

There's No Way—Lauv feat. Julia Michaels

Lost In Japan—Shawn Mendes & Zedd

When the Truth Hunts You Down—Sam Tinnesz

Slow Hands—Niall Horan

Dangerously—Charlie Puth

ACKNOWLEDGMENTS

To Massy…this is all your fault. Love you, boo!
Thanks to Danielle for saving me when I was drowning.

INTRO

A WAVE OF NAUSEA ROLLED THROUGH ME, AND ALL BECAUSE someone heated up some sausage in the break room. It was a smell that would have normally had my stomach growling, but not the past week. My stomach clenched before heaving up my breakfast and expelling it into the toilet.

"Nat, you okay?" my best friend, Jenna, asked as she knocked on the stall door.

I hastily wiped at my mouth and flushed the toilet as I stood. "Yeah." I turned the lock to find Jenna's dark brown eyes staring at me, a toothbrush and toothpaste in her hand.

"I love you," I said as I took them from her.

"You look like shit."

"I feel like it." My stomach clenched again, but I managed to breathe through it. Thanks to my actions that night, I was now swallowing back waves of nausea.

"Can you cancel the meeting?"

I shook my head. "No."

Jenna was always prepared, and I was very thankful to be able to wash my mouth out. I watched her reflection in the mirror as she pursed her lips, then pulled the hair band from her wrist. She took hold of my long, straight brown hair and manhandled it until it was a perfectly coiffed ponytail. Using her fingers, she pulled at some of the strands on top, lifting the front a bit.

I finished brushing and took the offered lipstick while she pinched my cheeks.

"I hate when you do that," I said as I straightened my sweater and adjusted my skirt.

"You look like the dead. I'm trying to bring some life into your skin."

She was right, and it definitely did help. "Thanks." I turned and stepped through the door and back to my desk to gather my binder for the meeting with the finance executives.

"Are you going to tell me what is going on?" Jenna asked as she followed me. Her own desk sat a few from mine.

My phone chose that moment to go off, a random number crossing the screen.

Happy Valentine's Day

It was the second vague message I'd gotten from the strange number in recent weeks, but there was never more information or anything to identify the sender, so I brushed it off.

"Not right now." I picked up the binder along with a notepad and pen and turned to head to where the meeting was beginning in a few short minutes.

She grabbed hold of my arm, the normal mirth in her eyes clouded with concern. For days she'd known something was wrong, and it was obvious she wasn't letting me brush it off anymore. "You've been spazzing all week long. Spill."

I huffed and looked around to make sure no one was listening before leaning in. "Not now."

"Babe, I'm worried about you and—"

"I'm pregnant."

Her eyes widened as she stared at me. "Wait, what?"

"You heard me." I turned and started walking toward the conference room, but Jenna was hot on my heels.

"How? When? Why didn't you tell me?"

I blew out a breath. Talking about my surprise pregnancy in the office was not the best plan. However, Jenna had caught me throwing up in the bathroom and helped me fix myself up again. It wasn't like I was keeping it from my best friend—I was going to tell her at breakfast tomorrow, not in the middle of the work day.

The news was still fresh to me, and I was processing and coming to terms with it while trying to figure out if there was any way I could find the father. My heart sank with that thought, one I'd tried my best to keep away, to keep from feeling the loss of something that could have been.

One magical, glorious night with quite possibly the man of my dreams, but I hadn't heard from him since and I had no way to contact him. Not even a last name. And I felt like an idiot because of it.

I had given him my number before we parted, but maybe he didn't feel the level of connection I did. Which only made my situation worse, because I wanted more than one night and I'd been certain he did too.

"New Year's Eve." It was cryptic, but she was also the only one who would understand, the only one in the building who had been there.

Her eyes popped wide. "Richard? Seriously?"

I nodded and continued on the path toward the conference room. Richard, with his devilish smile, perfectly styled brown hair, and vibrant blue eyes. Strong arms and wicked wit to combat my own. A gentleman at his core and an attraction neither of us could deny. Combined with the wit, it created some very flirtatious conversations—that then led to him between my thighs.

"I can't believe you got knocked up on New Year's Eve!" Jenna whisper yelled as we passed through the entrance to the conference room.

"Jenna!" I hissed, glaring at her.

She slapped her hand over her mouth once she realized we were no longer alone. "Oh my God," she mumbled through her fingers.

The whole room had heard, and all chatter ceased. Great.

My jaw clenched tight and I drew in a deep breath before turning to the room full of executives. It was my first meeting with them in my new position as a supervisor of accounting and acting manager while my manager, Nina, was, ironically, on maternity leave.

Most of the room had come down from Chicago, and I'd already made the worst first impression possible. Turning toward them, I made sure my head was held high, ignoring what Jenna just exposed for all to hear.

Some gazes moved awkwardly from me and I was ready to move on to the meeting, but I froze at the sight of the man sitting at the head of the table. Our eyes locked, and I felt mine widen. His did as well, but then he quickly schooled his expression, though I did notice that his lips were still parted in surprise.

"Natasha?"

"Richard?" I stared at him in absolute stunned shock. It was him. The man of my dreams and father of the spawn brewing inside me had a last name, and he was none other than Richard Bennett, VP of Finance. My boss's boss's boss's boss.

Shit!

The room was silent as we stared at each other. His eyes flickered to my abdomen and stayed there for a moment before meeting mine again. "Happy Valentine's Day?"

A harsh laugh left me. "We'll see about that."

"Dinner? Seven?" he asked, and I knew it was an acknowledgement of what Jenna said.

The other executives' gazes whipped between us in confusion.

"Sounds wonderful." I gave him a tight smile. All the while, my heart slammed inside my chest in a combination of fear, anxiety, and a flutter of hope. He remembered me. I wasn't forgettable. Not only that, he immediately wanted to see me, and somehow, I knew it wasn't simply for the new information Jenna had just thrown out.

Seeing him again made me instantly remember everything about *that night*...

PART 1

New Year's Eve

I STARED AT MY REFLECTION, ANALYZING EVERY ANGLE. My light hazel eyes popped out from the smoky eye makeup, and my face was framed by what I called miracle curls of my coffee-colored hair. Perfectly pink lips with a hint of mischief finished the look.

The silver off-the-shoulder dress with its flared skirt was festive, along with a mix of cute and sexy. Best thing—pockets.

While I did have a wristlet, I could use the pockets as well. The silver wristlet had just enough room for my phone, lipstick, and some cards and cash.

"How do I look?" I asked as I stepped out of the hotel bathroom.

Jenna's lips twitched up into a smile. "Like a hot beotch." She slipped a silver bangle over her hand. "Zip me up?"

I stepped over as Jenna turned, the glitzy deep red of her fitted dress contrasting against her golden, fair skin. Like mine, her dress sparkled in the light.

Chicago's Resolution Gala was all about the shiny. It was an event we'd both looked forward to for months—the ultimate year-end party. We booked a few nights at the W Hotel with a room overlooking the lake that included a great view of the pier, which was already lit up.

Earlier in the day, the drive up to Chicago from Indianapolis had been filled with car karaoke and a growing buzz of excitement for the evening's event.

Jenna picked at my hair, fixing a few strands that were bound to be decimated in minutes, but still, she'd spent a considerable amount of time styling it. My hair was normally stick straight and fought every single curl, but Jenna didn't back down. Her black hair was silky and about as straight as mine, so she knew how to make it submit.

"I think we're ready." She picked up her phone and hit a few keys before throwing it down on the bed.

A couch lined the wall under the window, and I sat there as I slipped on my black platform shooties—a combo of heeled sandals and booties. As I stood, I was suddenly four inches taller.

"I wish I was this tall all the time," I lamented.

Jenna quirked a brow, her own four-inch heels still keeping her an inch shorter than me. "And you could be if you wore those every day."

"I meant without them, smartass."

"But just think how banging your legs would look all the time."

We pulled on our coats so at least part of us would be warm out in the cold of winter in the windy city, and headed down to the lobby.

"Uber is almost here," Jenna said as she looked down at her phone. "Ready?"

"Ready."

The drive was a short one, but the line for drop-offs was nearly as long as the pier itself. Thankfully it continued to move at a fairly steady rate. It was way too cold out to walk, especially wearing a dress.

A gust of frigid air swept across my bare legs as I stepped out of the car and I cried out, hurrying my way to the entrance. We presented our tickets, then dropped our coats off at the coat check. With each step, my smile grew and the excitement pumped harder through my veins.

I felt as if my whole face lit up as I looked around in awe. The large dome structure was huge and already bursting with people. Lights of all colors moved around the room and up the dome walls, the music pumping through speakers. The deep bass beats shook the air, higher notes speeding up my blood as they pulsed through me.

"Oh, yeah, tonight is going to be trouble," Jenna said as she scanned the room. A man in a suit was her weakness—mine too—and there were hundreds of them.

"Hell. Yes." We high-fived and made our way to the closest bar.

Jenna ordered two vodka cranberries and we decided to move away from the entrance to a less crowded area.

Each step was a half dance—impossible to refuse the music and the movement it demanded.

Between the music and the throngs of people, it took a few minutes to cross the great space. Then finally, we found a spot and paid homage to the DJ and his sick beats.

I let go, eyes closed, arms up, every inch of my body surrendering to the beat. There was no pause, each song rolling into the next with fluid precision. Jenna and I sang, and sometimes screamed, along with the lyrics.

"I'm out," she said, pointing to her empty cup. I finished off the last few sips of mine, and we located the nearest bar for a refill.

We retrieved our cups and headed back to the area we'd been in when one of the many bodies around us turned suddenly and stepped into me. Everything moved very slow and very fast at the same time.

The wave of red was vivid before it suddenly splashed down all over the front of my dress.

"Shit! I'm so sorry."

My mouth popped open wide, back hunched with my arms wide in an effort to keep the liquid from my skin. Before me was a black suit with a grey button-down. As I worked my way up, a strong jaw appeared, followed by a set of kissable lips, a slightly crooked nose, and brilliant blue eyes that almost glowed in the low light and made my heart skip. Considering how far I had to crane my neck to see the guy, I could tell he was easily over six feet, and he was staring at me like he was waiting.

"Shit," was all I could manage before I scrunched my eyes and glanced down. The once silver cloth was stained with red.

"I need to go wash this."

"Let me help," he said.

I blinked at him, wondering how he was going to help but not willing to say no because he was too good looking. One of those types you wouldn't kick out of bed unless he said he was better on the floor.

I nodded and looked to Jenna, who mysteriously didn't come to the rescue and offer to help. She grinned at me like the Cheshire Cat. "You better go take care of that before it sets. We'll find someone to clean this up," she said with a wink.

He held out his hand to help me step away from the pool of liquid and ice at my feet. Once we were a few feet away I thought he would release my hand, but instead he held it tightly as we moved through the mass of people.

We found the restrooms, and I was happy that there was one for families spaced between the men's and women's.

"Perfect," he said as he held the door open, making sure to lock it behind him.

Inside was a good-sized space with plenty of room and a large counter and sink.

Immediately he began wetting paper towels while I pulled dry ones down. He took hold of the stack in my hand before I could say anything and shoved them down the front of my dress, holding them there. My eyes went wide and I drew in a sharp breath in shock at having some strange man's hand invade my space like that.

My muscles coiled to slap him, but there was something very clinical about his actions, the crease in his brow as he manipulated the towels, and that stopped me. He had the wet ones pressed against the fabric and was using the dry ones underneath to soak up the moisture. It took about two seconds for the realization to dawn, and his eyes bugged out of his head before meeting my startled gaze.

"I am so sorry."

"About the drink, or about shoving your hand down a strange woman's dress?"

"Both, but definitely the latter." Instead of pulling his hand out, he continued to dab against the fabric. It should have been awkward, but I found it more humorous than anything. "This is how I get stains out of my shirts before they set," he said by way of an explanation.

I started to giggle, and he began to chuckle. There was a sparkle in his eyes that drew me in. "At least it wasn't the bottom of my dress."

"I definitely would have been rightfully slapped."

"Or junk punched. I mean, I don't even know your name and you're already at second base."

His smile was wide, exposing a perfect row of white teeth. "Hi, I'm Richard. It's nice to meet you."

I bit down on my bottom lip. "Hi, Richard. I'm Natasha."

His eyes left mine and focused on his hands where he was blotting. "I think I got most of it." He pulled a few more dry towels out, replacing the wet ones to pull out some moisture. "When it dries, you shouldn't be able to tell."

A gasp left me as his fingers brushed against my breasts when he pulled his hand out.

He cleared his throat and stepped back, the air noticeably thick between us. The heaviness was something I hadn't felt in ages, and it was off to experience it with a man I'd first seen not more than fifteen minutes ago.

I turned to the mirror to look at my dress, a darker silver replacing the red and even that was beginning to fade. "Wow, neat trick. I'll have to remember that. I'm always feeding my shirt at lunch."

"And all wiping at it does is spread it everywhere."

"So true." There was an ease that I wasn't expecting, a calm, like I'd known him for years. "Thank you for your help, Richard."

"Anytime," he said, his lips twitching up into a smirk. "Thank you for not slapping me."

"I almost did, and you never know. The night is still young." I reached out and swatted at his ass, which was deliciously muscular.

"I amend my statement—thank you for not slapping my face. You are welcome to slap my ass as much as you want."

"Masochist."

He took my hands and placed them on his chest. "I'm a masochist for wanting your hands on my body?"

I drew in a shaky breath. There was a definite current passing between us that wanted more. "Wow, we should get back out there before I do something I have never done before and will probably regret in the morning."

"You're right. We should remain chaste and pure and not give in to these lustful thoughts." He held the door open and ushered me through. The music wasn't as intense in the hallway as the main room, so we stayed back.

"Who said they were lustful?" I asked. It had been a while since I'd flirted with a guy, let alone one that gave as good as he got.

"I assumed that 'something' you were thinking of was my same 'something' I was thinking and that, while I probably wouldn't regret it in the morning, there is a fair chance I'll want more."

I quirked a brow at him. "More than a night? We just met."

"A phone number at the very least."

I pursed my lips at him, though I was pretty sure I would give him my number. "Hmm, let's see how the night goes."

"Does that mean you'll be my dance partner for the evening?" he asked and held out his hand.

I slipped mine in his and let out a gasp at the current that passed between us. "Oh, I feel like we're at some high school formal now. All I need is a corsage, booze pilfered from my parents' lacking at-home bar, and awkward teenage sex, and the night is complete."

The crease reappeared in his brow. "I'd like to think my performance has improved since prom."

I shrugged my shoulders. "I have no basis for a comparison other than my own experiences and—" I drew a breath in through my teeth "—there are no lost world wonders there."

He leaned his shoulder against one of the massive columns. "I can't tell if the bar is really low or if your expectations are extremely high."

"Can you make a woman come?" I asked with a quirk of my brow.

"It's been a while, but the deed would have my full attention." His tongue peeked out to wet his lips.

I mimicked his stance, leaning against the wide base, facing him. "That's enough to be a consideration. How long is a while?"

"How long is a while to you?" he countered.

"I had three dates with a guy around Valentine's Day, hoping to have some great love connection and not be alone on the biggest love-fest day of the year, but the sex put the nail in that coffin real quick."

"That bad?"

"I'm not sure he ever progressed past prom sex. Plus he barely had it in before he was coming."

"That is bad."

I twirled my hand in the air. "Hence my dry spell. Why do I need a guy when my vibe does a better job than any man ever has?"

That perfect grin appeared again. "That sounds like a challenge."

"Well, I know you have zero hesitation about shoving your hands into my clothes. Assertiveness is sexy." It was possibly the strangest first conversation I'd ever had with anyone, but I went with it simply because it flowed so well and he never approached or said anything in a sleazy manner.

"I wish my employees thought that. Then again, they're probably praying I get laid."

Our exchange had twisted, and I wanted an answer to my question before we veered off course. "So, how long was that while?"

His eyes were locked with mine, unfaltering as his lips ticked. "Two years."

My mouth dropped open. "No."

He held his hands up and pursed his lips. "I'm married to my job. Trust me, it's not for lack of desire or performance ability."

"That's a turnoff." I straightened and slipped my arms around his arm to pull us away. "Back to the people and the booze that hopefully will not end up on my dress again."

He held firm, causing me to turn and look at him. "Wait, what was a turnoff?"

"Married to your job."

"And why is that?"

I tilted my head to look at him, actually believing the two years and quite possibly a lack of women in his life, period. "Because my female brain is already releasing chemicals, making me think of you as more than a night."

"Chemicals?"

"Hormones, whatever." I waved my hand in front of me. "There's this attraction physically, and our banter is on point, making me like your personality more and more with each minute. That then transitions into wondering what happens after tonight. Will this be all? Because as is, I am already interested in getting to know you, which has me thinking about a future with you, because I'm not one of those live-in-the-moment types," I explained.

"I'm not either."

"Then you said that, and a bucket of cold water rushed over me because those thoughts of something more were extinguished as soon as I understood there would be no room for anything more in your world than tonight."

He stared into my eyes, unblinking. "You are so interesting."

My brow scrunched and I glared at him. "I hate that word."

"Why?" he asked.

"Because it can go so many ways." Both good and bad, and I never knew how it was meant.

"I thought the inflection of my voice would be a giveaway that it was a good interesting. I'm quite in awe of you. And to clarify—I'm married to my job because I don't have anyone in my life. There is nothing but loneliness when I walk into my house."

The last sentence hit way too close to home, but at least I had Jenna. "Friends?"

He shrugged. "They all have families or live far away."

"No kids for you?"

He shook his head. "Not yet."

"Hmm." I stared out the window at the lake, watching as a party boat set off from the pier. On board was a mirror image to what was happening inside the ballroom where we stood.

"Now what's going on in that interesting brain of yours?" he asked with a tug on my hand.

"Nothing."

"I've known you for less than an hour, and I already know it's not nothing."

The man was observant, driven, witty, courteous, and sexy as fuck. And that was just what I'd picked up in a short time. "Another tick in the you-are-too-good-to-be-true column. Are you a serial killer?"

He threw his head back in laughter. "I do have flaws. Thankfully not of the serial killer variety."

I narrowed my gaze on him. "Hmm, I'm not so sure you have any so-called flaws."

"You know nothing about me," he pointed out.

That was a challenge if I'd ever heard one. Time to test him and his interest level while showing just how observant I was.

"You're a workaholic who probably orders food in every day or has one of those meal delivery box services. Some big condo that overlooks the lake, devoid of personality or comfort. Your employees dislike and respect you at the same time."

"How did you know I live in Chicago, let alone have a condo

that overlooks the lake? Are you stalking me?" His expression was a mix of curiosity and suspicion.

A laugh left me. "I don't even know your last name, so that's a no. And a man who is married to his job isn't going to go on a road trip for a New Year's Eve party. You'll probably sleep in tomorrow and then work from home in the afternoon while downing coffee like it's life."

Suspicion and curiosity were quickly replaced with awe. "If we hadn't met by absolute chance, I would be seriously freaked out by how accurate you are."

I gave him a shrug and a smirk. "It's a gift."

"All I've gotten is that you are beautiful and sexy and quite possibly the most perceptive person I've ever met."

"That's it?"

"And you can hold your own in possibly any conversation or situation. But I'd like to know more than that, and more than how fucking fantastic sex would be with you."

"You think it would be that good?" I asked, though I had the same feeling.

"Don't you?"

I tugged on his hand. "Let's go dance and find out."

We stopped at one of the thirty bars located around the party on our way back to the area where we'd left Jenna. Richard replaced my drink while getting himself a beer. I took a few quick sips before we moved through the crowd.

Bodies gyrated everywhere, the crowd at max energy. It took some weaving until I located Jenna's familiar form dancing with a couple of people not far from where we left her.

"Keenan," Richard called out.

A very handsome black man with a megawatt smile turned at the sound, but didn't stop dancing with Jenna.

"What happened, man?" he asked, glancing over to me.

"Wardrobe malfunction."

"And you were being a gentleman helping the lady out?" He gave me a wink.

"He was a perfect gentleman." It wasn't a lie. While our conversation had been full of innuendos and highly sexually charged banter, physically his focus was on helping me and making certain I was okay.

"All good?" Jenna asked, giving Richard an appraising once-over before mouthing to me, "He's hot."

I mouthed back, "I know," before Richard caught my attention again.

"Natasha, this is my friend Keenan. Keenan, Natasha."

Keenan held out his hand, that megawatt smile still covering his face. "Nice to meet you."

I slipped my hand in his. "Same."

"So you do have friends," I said to Richard.

He chuckled. "A few."

Jenna whipped around to me when a remix of "Heathens" came on, and immediately we began belting out the lyrics and jumping to the beat. Richard and Keenan eventually joined in, both showing off some skillful moves, especially Keenan.

The DJ was good, keeping the energy in the room up, mixing familiar songs with electric beats. Each song rolled effortlessly into the next, and we never stopped. The lights zipped across the crowd in brilliant colors, refracting off any shiny surface.

Smiles lit up every face as everyone let go, if only for a few hours.

Turning to Richard, I smiled and locked eyes with him as I tipped my cup back and gulped down the last of my vodka and cranberry.

"We have some catching up to do."

He nodded his head, then followed suit. "Another?" he asked once his cup was empty. I nodded, and he looked to Jenna. "Refill?"

Her eyes went wide and she nodded. "Thank you!"

"I'll help," Keenan said and they stepped away, leaving us to stay lost in the beat.

"There are major sparks going on between you two," Jenna said as she fanned herself.

"Trust me, I know."

"Did you fuck in the bathroom?" she asked.

My mouth popped open. "What? No!"

She shrugged. "You were gone so long, I figured that's what was going on."

"Minutes after literally bumping into me?"

She waggled her eyebrows. "I would have."

"I don't know what is going on," I said.

"What do you mean?" she asked.

"We've had this instant connection. I feel like I've known him for years, not to mention the sexual chemistry, which is…wow."

She bounced with excitement. "You have my permission to go get it, girl. I am good."

Jenna was a social butterfly so I had no doubt about that, but I wasn't sure I could do it.

Richard and Keenan returned, drinks in hand, and passed them out.

"Do I need to test this?" Jenna asked, and both men stared at her in confusion. "You know, for drugs?" Both men's eyes widened as they adamantly shook their heads in protest. "Good. Thank you."

Richard leaned in. "What is she talking about?"

I reached into my wristlet and pulled out a key fob with a white disc. "Date rape drug tester."

His mouth dropped open. "I didn't know such a thing existed."

I nodded. "Yup. Jenna loves to go dancing, and she's been slipped a few in the past. Luckily there was always someone she trusted close by to take care of her. As soon as they came on the market, she bought a ton and insisted I carry one around."

"That's damn smart and a good thing to have." He leaned in closer. "Just so you know, I would never do anything like that."

I bumped his shoulder with mine. "I think we both know you don't need anything like that with me."

He bumped me back. "If I do, I've been reading this whole night wrong."

We went back to dancing, and at some point a group of people came up—people who obviously knew Richard and Keenan. Jenna and I paid no attention and continued to dance.

When my third drink was empty and I was feeling tipsy, I leaned in toward Jenna.

"I'm hungry!" I yelled to her. "Feed me, woman!"

She continued to dance as she pointed to the wall where the buffet was set up.

I glared at her. "You don't love me."

A kissy face was all the response I got before she used the dance to conceal pointing behind me.

Richard glanced at me from a group of guys he was talking to, a smile on his face.

I used my first finger to point to my open mouth. Oddly, his eyes widened. After a few quick words, he stepped over to me.

"You want to give me a blow job?" he asked.

My eyes widened in horror. "No! Oh my God is that what… it's the international 'feed me' symbol."

"And with our conversations tonight, I took it as 'feed me your cock.'"

I shook my head. "You have to deliver before that happens. It's not all about you."

A chuckle left him, and he nodded. "Deal."

"I'm starving."

He nodded in agreement. "Let's grab some plates and go upstairs."

I shook my head. "That's VIP seating."

"Yes, it is."

I stared at him, openmouthed. "You've got a table on the balcony?"

"Yes."

"Lead the way, Mr. VIP."

The buffet spread was huge, and I began to wonder why we hadn't been before. I loaded my plate, Richard in step behind me.

"Are you copying me?" I asked as he took the tongs from me.

He glanced at my plate and chuckled at the matching items. "Not intentionally."

Some flatbreads, cheese, veggies, potatoes, meats, and dips filled both our plates as we made our way upstairs.

Richard flashed his ticket, and the guard stepped aside to let us through. It was quite a walk around the balcony until he stopped at a four-topper and set our plates down. The view of the crowd was insane. Nothing but a mash of bodies in flashes of light in the dark. I was kind of happy to have the brief reprieve.

My feet let out a groan of appreciation when I sat, giving them the first bit of relief in hours.

"Wow, these are great seats," I said.

"Keenan is to thank for that. It was his idea that we get a table."

"So, who is Keenan?" I asked with a laugh before crunching on a carrot stick.

"A friend," he said before taking a bite of one of the flatbreads.

"Well, I gathered that."

He chuckled and finished chewing. "We met in college and both ended up in Chicago. What about Jenna?"

"We met at my first job after college, became fast friends, and have been inseparable ever since." I moved on to one of the flatbread pieces, pleasantly surprised by the pop of the unexpected combination of sweet and savory.

"What do you do when you're not bumping into strange men and having their hand down your dress in less than five minutes?"

I threw my head back in laughter. "Total numbers nerd—I work in accounting."

It was his turn to laugh. "Finance."

"You're kidding." He shook his head. "Another tick for Mr. Too-Good-To-Be-True."

He laughed while biting on one of the potatoes. "I'm a numbers nerd as well. I have an unhealthy relationship with spreadsheets."

My mouth popped open. "I love spreadsheets. Like, legit obsession. Spreadsheets are life."

He leaned forward conspiratorially. "Do you love pivot tables as much as I do?"

A shudder rolled through me. "Stop talking nerdy to me. I already liked you before I found out about the nerdy side of your athlete-in-a-suit disguise."

"What?"

I waved my hand in his direction. "Hide the muscles all you want, but that ass says differently," I said with a wink.

He shrugged. "I think best in the gym when my mind is occupied, and since I've already told you how I'm a lonely bastard, pretty much all of my free time is spent there."

"So you can peacock on these rare nights out?"

He smirked and shook his head. "I was a high school football player, you got me there. Got a football scholarship to college and not halfway through my freshman year, I was injured. Keeping my strength up helps keep the pain away."

It was quite possibly the most serious thing said all evening, and damn if it didn't endear me to him further. "What happened?"

He finished his bite and wiped his mouth. "I intercepted a pass and was booking it toward the goal. I made it thirty yards before I was tackled by two players and we went down wrong. Broken leg, broken elbow." He pointed to his right leg and left elbow. "End of a dream."

"Did they not heal right?" I couldn't even imagine the depth of despair that would create.

He shook his head. "It took two surgeries to fix my tibia, and one for the elbow. They were both fucked. It took years for me to figure out how to manage them so that I'm not popping pills all the time for the rest of my life. What about you?"

"No football injuries for me."

Another chuckle before he speared a piece of cheese. "Sports?"

"Does riding my bike count? Or spending my summer in the

pool?" I asked. "I did play some sports, but I only got as far as high school freshman softball. My brother is the sporty one. He went on to minor league baseball. Plays for the Indians."

"Cleveland?" he asked, impressed but confused, as the Cleveland Indians were major league.

I shook my head. "Indianapolis Indians. They're a triple-A team."

"That's cool."

"Otherwise, my favorite form of exercise just isn't happening lately." I didn't mean to steer what was a neutral, good, get-to-know-you kind of conversation back to sex, but watching him bite into a strawberry and lick the juice from his lips was more than I could take.

"Of the naked variety?"

"Of course, but like I said, not happening." I let out a sigh and tried to redirect again. "So I spend the most boring hour a day on the elliptical machine with the music blaring so loud it pisses my neighbors off. I hate apartment living."

"Poor sound insulation," he said in a knowing tone.

I nodded. "Too right. I mean, one reason it's so loud is because they're both screaming."

His plate was mostly demolished, as was mine. The food settled, my stomach happy to have something besides liquid in it.

"I've lived with neighbors like that, always fighting," he said.

I shook my head. "Oh, no. They're not fighting. They fuck like twenty-four seven." His eyes met mine, and I realized I'd done it again. "Doesn't matter anyway. I'll be out of there in a few months."

"Another apartment?"

I pulled out my phone and brought up the listing for a property I'd had my eye on. "Me and Jenna are both looking at this condo complex downtown on the river. We can be neighbors."

His brow scrunched as he looked over the photos. "Wait, where do you live?" he asked.

"Indianapolis."

His lips formed a thin line. "Damn, I wish you lived here."

His wish made my heart jump and my chest clench. I was buzzing with the idea of seeing him after tonight. "I hooked you already, did I?" I tried to play off how much I liked the idea.

"You've had me since I shoved my hand down your dress. Nice breasts, by the way." He winked at me.

I rolled my eyes and shook my head. "Well, Indianapolis isn't far, and therefore, neither are my breasts."

He stared at me, studying me for a moment. "How are you single?"

Given his scrutiny, that was not what I was expecting.

I blinked at him. "How are you? I mean, I'm a weird, numbers-obsessed, nerd hottie. Guys get so confused they don't know if they like me or just want sex. You're a straight-up god-like man… I'm still trying to find a flaw."

"I'm scarred. That's a flaw."

I shook my head. "That just makes you more perfect."

"You're pretty flawless yourself, you know," he said as he set his hand on mine.

I bit down on my bottom lip and looked away, but he wouldn't let me. He hooked his finger under my chin and made me look at him. "I wasn't going to come out tonight, but I'm really glad I did. And I'm even more glad I bumped into you and spilled your drink all over your dress." His eyes grew heavy and he cleared his throat before standing. "Let's go dance."

He held out his hand and I slipped mine in, rising back up. "What just happened there?"

He pulled me closer until our bodies were aligned. Electric heat poured through me when his arms wrapped around my waist, hands spread across my back. My heart sped up to triple time.

Leaning forward, he bent down and ran his nose up the column of my neck, his lips at my ear. A shudder ran through me, and I leaned farther into him. The desire to be skin to skin with him was strong.

"My mind went to the gutter and I was consumed with wanting to spill another fluid all over you. Inside you."

"Fuck," I hissed as my knees went weak, my fingers fisting his shirt.

"Now, I need to get you onto the dance floor before I steal you away to my place to ring in the New Year."

That was such an appetizing proposition, and as much as my body wanted to convince him that was the right move, I knew it wasn't. Despite Jenna's opinion, which was for me to go get it. "Let's go."

The group that included Jenna and Keenan had grown, new friends and old having joined. I recognized a guy I'd gone to college with.

"Brent!" I cried out.

"Hey, little Nat," he said, stepping forward and pulling me into a hug, lifting me from the ground before setting me back down and moving away. He was still as tall and lanky as I remembered, and at least six inches taller than Richard. "Long time. What have you been up to?"

I shrugged. "Work, and hanging out with her."

Brent glanced over to Jenna who smiled and waved at us, shaking her ass and hips. I was beginning to wonder how she was still standing. Then again, she loved to dance.

"Jenna's your friend?" he asked.

I narrowed my gaze at him. "Yeah. Why?"

"Because I like her."

"Because she's Japanese?" Brent always did have a thing for Asian girls.

His lips twitched up into a smirk. "That may be part of it. So who's the guy you came over with?"

I glanced over to Richard, who was talking with Keenan but kept glancing over to me. I crooked my finger at him, and he closed the few feet that separated us.

"Brent, this is Richard. Richard, this is an old college friend, Brent."

"Nice to meet you." Richard held out his hand and Brent took it.

"How long have you two been together?" Brent asked.

"We just met tonight," I answered.

Brent's brow scrunched and he looked between us, at the way Richard's arm sat loosely around my waist. "Really?"

"Yes."

"Fooled me," he said.

I stole a glance at Richard, who was smiling at me.

"Come back, Brent!" Jenna called out.

A smile broke out on his face. "Gotta dance." His hips began to shake to the beat as he backed up until he bumped Jenna.

Richard drew me closer, his mouth near my ear. "I was starting to get a little jealous there."

I angled my face toward his. "Jealous? Really?"

His thumb stroked against my waist. "I seem to have claimed you as mine tonight, and here is this other guy who is friendly with you."

I turned in his arms, my hands resting on his chest. "Oh, claimed me as yours."

"What?"

I nipped at his jaw. "Definite turn-on, in both words and possibility."

A groan left him. "You are going to kill me."

"Kill you how?"

He returned my nip with one of his own. "Death by constant erection."

Heat flooded my face and I glanced down, but between the darkness and the fabric, I couldn't see anything. Taking hold of my hips, he spun me around and used the music and dancing as an excuse to grind against me.

"Oh," I said in surprise before reaching up and cupping his neck.

We were in our own little world, moving to the music, our

lips drawing closer. Before we could connect, Jenna yelled out, breaking the spell of our bodies.

"Woohoo! Get it!" She laughed.

Keenan followed suit, giving a whistle. "Damn, Rick."

Richard chuckled against my neck before reluctantly creating space between us. The energy that moved around us was intoxicating. I'd never been so turned on and desperate for any man.

Neither of us was interested in anyone or anything else going on. It was like as soon as our eyes had met, we were hooked on some chemical level. All conversation throughout the evening only intensified the feeling.

A remix of Lykke Li's "Little Bit" pumped through the speakers. The words rang out as Richard and I danced, our fingers linking together.

In that moment, I was a little bit in love with him.

Was it real? No, but for the moment, it felt real. The interest in knowing more about him was there, and I was desperate for more information but was silenced by every cell in my body calling out for his. The need to know his hands on my skin was a desperation that demanded action.

"I'll go get us some drinks," he said after a few highly charged songs.

"Can you get me a Cosmo?"

When he returned I greedily gulped down the liquid, desperate to quench my thirst, which wasn't the best idea.

Shortly thereafter I swayed on my feet. "I have to go to the bathroom," I said to Richard.

He leaned in. "I'll take you."

"That's a little weird." I looked over to Jenna, who was completely wrapped up with Brent. I didn't want to pull her away from that.

"After everything that's happened tonight, you think that is weird?"

I shrugged, and my foot wobbled a little on the heel. Richard grabbed my arm to steady me, and I fell against his chest.

"Okay, you can help me," I relented. The wobble only highlighted the ache in my feet that I'd successfully ignored since we ate.

"Thought so."

I patted his chest. "You just don't want to lose sight of me."

"In this crowd?" he asked. "No. Remember, you're my dance partner tonight."

I angled my head back. "I want to be more than that."

He brushed my hair back behind my ear, his gaze locked with mine. "Much more." He took my hand and guided us to the restrooms, but instead of releasing me, he tugged me back into the family restroom.

"Fuck, my feet hurt," I whined as I leaned against the handrail. They throbbed, and even the slight release of some weight helped. I forgot about the pain while dancing, but without the distraction, it hit me full force.

Richard's eyes trailed down my legs to my heels, then back up, stopping at the hem of my dress. In one smooth motion he stepped forward, leaned down, and hooked his hands to the back of my thighs, lifting me from the ground. A squeak of shock left me as his hands trailed up, slipping under my dress until he was cupping my ass. My legs spread without thought, crossing around his waist as his hips pinned me to the wall.

"Better?" he asked, his lips no more than a few inches from mine.

"That wasn't exactly what I had in mind, but it works."

"What did you have in mind?" His gaze flickered to my lips, then back up.

My lips twitched up into a smile and I flexed my legs. A gasp left me as the hard length of his cock pressed against my clit.

"You like bumping into me," I purred.

A groan left him, his hips flexing. "It's that magnetic pull you have. I just can't help myself."

"How did we end up in *this* bathroom again?" I asked.

"You needed an escort."

I quirked a brow. "To pee? Isn't it a little early in our relationship for you to be in the room for that? I mean, I know your hands are on my ass, but your lips haven't even—"

His lips crashed to mine, ending my sentence along with my incessant wondering of how his kiss would feel—spine-tingling, clit-pulsing, heat-spreading, glorious perfection.

A moan left me, my hips undulating against him as I ran my hands around his neck and wound my fingers into his soft hair. A moan vibrated in his chest and his kiss became harder, deeper, as he drew me impossibly closer, bending me until I surrendered all thoughts.

"How many people do you think have had sex in here tonight?" I asked when we parted.

His hips continued to rock against me, his teeth nipping at my bottom lip. "As long as I'm one of them, I don't give a fuck."

It wasn't what I wanted, but want was taking a backseat to need, and I needed him desperately.

A rattle of the handle and a pounding on the door jolted us back to awareness. "Somebody in there?"

A groan left him and his head fell down to my shoulder. With reluctance, he released me and set me back down on my feet.

With him spun around and the sink running, I finished what I'd come in to do, which was still weird with him there, and we stepped out, receiving curious glances from those outside.

"Why don't we go upstairs so you can sit down?"

I nodded as we walked. Each step was torture, but I pressed on until I found a little alcove between two of the large columns. The space was partially obstructed by a potted tree.

With a tug, we slipped into the small space and I leaned against the corner of the column and the window, which had a slight ledge. The darkness shielded us some from those walking by.

"Are you okay?"

I nodded. "Maybe the four-inch heels weren't the right choice for a long night."

"Well, if it makes a difference, I appreciate them," he said as his fingers skimmed against my thigh.

Oddly it did, and his touch only ignited my need for more.

"The fireworks are starting soon," I said.

"And?"

"My hotel isn't far."

He froze and stared at me for a moment. "Fuck, yes."

He started to pull me, and a hiss of pain left me as I stumbled. Strong arms caught me, drawing me closer and lifting me enough to take the pressure off.

"Sorry," he said.

"Eager much?" I reached out and pressed my hand against the hard line beneath the fabric of his suit.

"Does that answer your question?" he asked with a low groan.

I wrapped my fingers as far around as the fabric allowed, earning a low groan as he sagged into me. "It's a pretty good indicator."

"Do you think you can walk? That dress is too short for me to carry you, and there are too many people bumping around for you to take your shoes off."

I drew him closer until his lips were on mine. One brief touch and I was pinned between his body and the brick wall. Electric tingles danced across my skin from each point of contact.

"Your dick is doing all the thinking," I whispered.

"Says the woman who is grabbing onto my ass and pulling me closer, rubbing her body against mine."

I pressed my lips against his neck, then nipped the spot with my teeth. "I blame you."

After hours of flirting and touching, we were both out of our minds with want.

"Fuck," he hissed. His hand disappeared under the edge of my dress, and I drew in a sharp breath when his fingers pressed against my clit. My eyes were locked with his, both of us lost as his fingers slipped beneath the edge of my thong and across my slick opening. His eyes grew darker, heavier. "You're so wet."

A low moan left me as two fingers slipped between my folds. It wasn't the body part I was aching for, but all that mattered was that he was touching me.

He worked his fingers hard, his body blocking me from view. I bit down on the lapel of his jacket to keep from crying out as he slapped against my clit with each thrust of his fingers that were drilling into me. My muscles locked down, but my knees turned weak. Richard kept me up with one strong arm wrapped around my waist.

A frustrated growl left him, and he withdrew his hand. Before I could protest, he spun me around and knotted his hand in my hair, pulling back and to the side before biting down on my shoulder, no longer a man but an animal fueled by lust.

My mouth popped open, vision fuzzy while my pussy clenched in desperation.

His fingers returned, answering my call, and picked up in pace, furiously moving in and out with purpose. I didn't even notice he'd released my hair until I felt cool fingers against my tight nipple after his hand slid down the front of my dress.

"Oh my God," I hissed, unable to keep my keening locked away.

"You make the hottest sounds." His hand clamped down on my breast, using it as an anchor point, pinching my nipple between two fingers.

The added sensation quickly had me on edge with his relentless momentum. My head fell back against his shoulder, back arched, one hand pressed against the brick while the other reached back to fist his hair.

"R—" My breath hitched, muscles tense. "Richard."

Everything became fuzzy, my whole body tense, and then I crashed. There was no holding back my sounds or the rocking as each pulse slammed through me.

His fingers slowed while my shaking subsided. After removing them he spun me back around, holding me close, his forehead resting against mine.

I was still coming down from the intense orgasm he'd just given me.

He ground his teeth together as some semblance of rationality returned. "I need to get you home."

I shook my head and reached for his waist. "I can't wait."

"I don't have anything on me."

I pulled at his zipper and slipped my hand inside, sifting through the layers until I felt the hot silkiness of his cock. He jerked at the touch, his whole body shaking.

"Pull out."

Our breaths mingled and his gaze was clouded and lost to the singular purpose his body demanded, and so was I.

Frantically, he maneuvered his cock out through the hole made by the zipper and lifted my leg. He arranged my skirt to hide us before finding my opening and slamming in.

Every nerve lit up, a blaze of fire and electricity that burst from my core all the way to the top of my head and tips of my toes, before racing back. A second of pause and he pulled out, only to slam back in and send the sensation through me again when he bottomed out.

I'd never felt so full, so complete.

It was too much after just coming, and I clamped down on his neck to silence my moans. His breath was hard against my skin, fingers digging into my thigh as his frantic pace picked up.

I was lost in a sea of nothing but pleasure and the growing tension as I moved with him. A second orgasm slammed into me and I clamped down on him, my legs locking him all the way in. Spasms rocketed through me again, blinding white clouding my vision.

A strangled groan and a whispered "fuck" could be heard as he shuddered before frantically reaching between us. He was barely out before he was coming.

Warm droplets fell against my skin as his cock jerked, the hot head rubbing against me with each involuntary thrust of his hips.

In the background I heard the countdown going on before there was nothing but screams and cheers.

"Happy New Year, Richard," I whispered against his lips.

His breath was still harsh as he came down. "Happy New Year, Natasha."

I swept a few strands of his hair from his forehead. "Better?"

He nodded. "And you?" There was a tingle as his lips worked their way down my jaw. "Did I accomplish my task?"

"You don't know?" I asked as I ran my hands up and down his back.

He chuckled. "I counted twice."

"Once with your fingers, and right at the end when my pussy milked your cock."

Another groan. "I wanted to stay inside you so badly."

We stayed in our little bubble for a few minutes, relishing our hidden time alone.

"I guess we should get your coat now," he said. He pulled the handkerchief from his top pocket and swiped up the now cooled droplets from my skin before discreetly righting our clothing.

Sex had released the pressure, but with his words I knew that wasn't enough for him, just as it wasn't enough for me.

"I need to tell Jenna I'm leaving. She'll probably stay until closing."

I moved to step forward, but my legs gave out. Before I careened into the ground, I was swept up in Richard's arms.

"Whoa! I've got you," he said as he held me close, keeping me upright.

"All your fault," I whimpered. My legs were going to take a minute to recover. When was the last time I could say a guy did that? Richard definitely deserved a repeat performance.

A chuckle rumbled deep in his chest. "Damn straight."

"Don't get all cocky on me now."

"No, I was all cocky *in* you."

I shook my head and rolled my eyes. "That was bad."

"Was it?"

"Definitely."

"Hmm, I'll have to blame it on the slow return of blood to my brain."

I glanced down to his crotch. "There was an awful lot elsewhere."

We headed back to where our quasi group had spent the evening. Richard kept his arm around me, holding me close and taking on much of my weight. Halfway there, near the window, sat Jenna on the floor with Brent and a few others crouched and standing around her.

"Nat! There you are," Jenna called out. One of her shoes was off and her ankle was twice the size of normal.

I ran over to Jenna the best I could with Richard's assistance. Between my Jell-O legs and my dead feet, it wasn't an easy journey.

"What happened?" I asked as I leaned over. A little wobble of my own and Richard's strong hands were wrapped around my waist to help steady me.

"I drank and I danced and then I fell," she said with more than a few slurs, but a smile on her face. It wasn't surprising, considering I never saw her eat anything but there was always a drink in her hand.

The truth was, I would probably be in the same place if I hadn't met Richard, if he hadn't distracted me from everything and everyone.

"We should get you back to the hotel, babe," I said as I brushed the hair back from her face. I froze for a moment before looking up to Richard. There was disappointment there along with understanding.

He pressed his lips to my shoulder.

"Can we order room service?" she asked.

"Sure. I'm going to go get your coat," I said as I took her clutch from her and pulled out her ticket. "You stay here."

Richard helped me to the coat check and held me close as we waited in line.

"I'm sorry," I said.

"She needs you."

"And I need more of you."

He placed a kiss on my forehead. "Same, but I've been selfish enough with you tonight. You'll just have to promise me a rain check."

"I like that idea."

After retrieving the coats and returning, I threw Jenna's at Brent, who happily helped her into it.

My legs were steadier and I didn't require Richard's assistance anymore, but that didn't mean I didn't want him close. My feet still hurt, but I was able to push it out of my mind to help Jenna. His fingers laced with mine as we made our way through the crowd yet again. Brent followed behind, helping Jenna.

There was a line of taxis waiting in the drop-off zone, and Richard pulled open the back door of one so Brent could set Jenna inside. They both pulled out their phones as they chatted, giving me the opportunity to do something I really didn't want to do.

I stepped closer to Richard and he wrapped his arms around my waist.

"Will you be okay?" Richard asked as he brushed my hair behind my ear.

I nodded, my heart heavy. I didn't like the feeling. I didn't like leaving him. "I'm so sorry," I said, holding onto the open edges of his suit jacket and tugging.

"Me too." He pressed his lips against my forehead.

"I wasn't ready for tonight to end." My voice caught, and I dreaded him walking away.

"Did I earn your phone number?" he asked.

I smiled at him and patted his chest. "And a blow job," I said before rattling off my number.

He leaned forward and pressed his lips to mine with soft, languid kisses, savoring each second of connection. "I had a wonderful evening, Natasha."

"So did I."

The cab driver yelled out, asking if we were ready. Reluctantly we pulled apart.

"Jenna, get that ankle looked at as soon as you can," Richard said.

"Aye, Aye, Captain Richard!" She giggled before whispering to Brent and pulling him in for a kiss.

My chest hurt, and my heart begged for time to stop. Each inch that increased the gap between us felt the size of the Grand Canyon. With a pained expression, he turned to walk away.

"Richard!" I called out. He twisted back around just in time for me to fling myself into his arms. I crashed my lips to his. Our mouths parted for one last taste as he held me tightly to him.

"Happy New Year," I whispered against his lips.

"Happy New Year." We shared a soft kiss, then another, before I stepped away, our hands holding on, reaching out for those last seconds of connection.

As we pulled away, I watched as he took out his phone and typed at the screen, his gaze flickering back to the cab.

I should have gotten a picture with him.

It was a night I would never forget and a man to always remember. I didn't know what the future held, but I begged for him to be in it.

AFTER

Part 2

Chapter ONE

Six weeks had passed since I last laid eyes on him, and I couldn't help but notice the difference. The excitement, the life I saw more and more through that night, was gone. The light inside was replaced by the loneliness I'd also seen in him. All work and no play.

It was hard to keep my attention on what was being said, my gaze locked on him. His lips moved, but I heard none of the words, until his eyes were fixed on me. In fact, the whole room was. A jolt of panic kicked inside me.

"I'm sorry?" I asked, realizing my wandering mind had missed something important.

"I asked why there are so many discrepancies in the GL for January. They should have been addressed before month end, yet they are still hanging open."

It was something I knew was going to come up. All accounts were supposed to be balanced by month end, but there were two general ledgers that wouldn't balance and I was still investigating the reason why.

I cleared my throat, nervous energy vibrating through my veins. "I am still learning my new position as well as handling Nina's. I'm afraid there has been a harder than usual learning curve with no support."

"That's an excuse," he said coolly.

I straightened my spine. "It's an explanation. Nina's sudden bedrest has left a gap in knowledge. Then there is Trent's position that I just took over the first week of January. There is no guide for me here, no instructions, and I am working to correct the issues while still training my replacement. January is almost settled, and I'm trying to keep February on track."

"We are literally halfway through February. There are no excuses for our financials to still be unsettled from January."

The Richard before me was demanding and gave me no slack, which infuriated me. Now I understood why he said his employees didn't like him. The frustration was getting to me, my jaw clenching as my eyes watered.

"I worked seventy hours last week," I spat. "If you want this done, you'll either wait or find someone who can help me."

Richard's eyes were slits. "You have until Wednesday."

"Or what?"

The entire table watched as words volleyed between us. Our once flirtatious banter was now a back and forth of wills, and I wasn't backing down from his overbearing personality, VP or not. I knew him in a way nobody else at the table did, of that I was certain.

"We will see, depending on how things turn out on Wednesday."

The urge to slap him was strong, but it wasn't going to be his ass again. This time I wanted to slap him right across his smug face. I could already envision the perfect pink impression of my hand blossoming over his skin.

His attention strayed from me onto other topics, areas where he wanted improvement.

"I think that should do for now. Natasha, you stay," Richard said as the meeting adjourned.

My stomach clenched in anticipation of how this was going to go. When the last person filed out and the door shut, he stood and walked toward me.

His expression softened. "I'm sorry, but I couldn't treat the situation any differently than I would with any other employee."

I nodded in understanding. And I did understand, but that didn't mean I liked the treatment. "Some of the things you said on New Year's are suddenly perfectly clear."

His gaze flitted across my features. Tingles brushed my cheek as he reached to cup my face.

"You're real."

"As opposed to a fantasy?" I asked, forcing myself not to lean in to the touch as I desperately wanted to.

"I was beginning to think you were a torturous dream that I couldn't wake from."

"That doesn't sound like a good thing."

"I called."

My lips formed a thin line. "Sure you did."

"That's not a lie to placate you or to worm my way into your better graces." His gaze hardened. "Though I have to know—did you know who I was?"

I shook my head. "Despite my uncanny ability to pin you down, it didn't click until I saw you today."

He nodded. "It seems we have some things to discuss, unless I'm mistaken as to who the father is." He reached out and gently placed his hand over my abdomen. The action made my heart skip, then melt.

"Considering I've had sex one time in over a year, it's a pretty safe bet."

"I really called you," he reiterated.

I didn't want lies, and I glared up at him. "You can keep telling yourself that, Richard, but I don't believe it."

He pulled out his phone to a contact with my name. There were multiple phone calls and a few unanswered texts. I blinked at the screen, scanning the words, then to the top at the number.

Giving him my number had been a hurried event with no time to double check—two of the numbers were transposed. My mouth fell open and all the hurt faded away. He hadn't forgotten about me, but just like me, he couldn't find me.

"After the last text I decided you gave me a fake number," he said.

"2-0-2-3, not 2-2-0-3."

He glanced down at his screen. "Shit."

I took the phone from him and altered the contact, then texted myself. "There, now we're connected."

"We were always connected, the phone was just off the hook," he said with a sad smile.

Relief flooded me, and I couldn't stop myself from standing on the tips of my toes, cupping his face, and pulling it down until I could press my lips to his. Shock and surprise filled his eyes for a fraction of a second before his strong arms pulled me into him.

Every feeling from that night exploded into a streak of bright and colorful fireworks.

"Wow," I said when we separated.

"More," was all he got out before crashing his lips to mine again.

A hunger growled from deep inside him, a desperation for exactly what he wanted—more. It clawed and so did I, frenzied and out of control until we were both a panting mess.

"You..."

"Me?"

His lips ghosted mine, parting as our breath mingled. "I'm starving for you and I don't understand why."

I nipped at his bottom lip. "There's the Richard I know."

"The one you know?"

"Versus VP Richard. The Richard who is honest with what he wants. Greedy and affectionate."

"I want you in ways I don't understand."

"Same." We were still glued to each other and giving no thought to anything going on outside of our little bubble. "Now, where are we going to go to dinner tonight? It's Valentine's Day. Everywhere is going to be packed."

Not only that, it was Friday, and I had a feeling that would make things worse.

"Let me worry about that. Just give me your address."

"Are you saying I have to leave work on time? The VP might not be happy with that. He gave me an ultimatum."

The corner of his lips ticked up. "Let me talk to him. I don't think he will have a problem with you leaving on time."

"And taking Saturday off? Unless you aren't staying…"

"I already have a hotel booked for the weekend. If you think I'm letting you go that fast, you're sorely mistaken."

I stretched up, my mind filling with ways he could leave me sorely aching that I would definitely like, and I told him so. "Then leave me sorely aching by the time you go."

Warmth filled me when our lips touched again, and it felt like things might actually start looking up. That the situation, the pregnancy, might not be as daunting and frightening, because he was there to share it.

At least that was my hope.

I exited the conference room, leaving him there to continue working.

I couldn't keep the smile from my face as I walked back to my desk, or the light that filled me for the first time in days. The mounting work on my desk, his ultimatum, didn't faze me anymore, though I did seem to be in a bit of a Richard-induced trance when I sat down.

"Holy shit," Jenna hissed as she pulled the chair from the desk next to mine and sat inches from me. "What happened? I mean, he hasn't called you, but by the look of your lips there was some major making out happening in there."

My eyes popped and I covered my mouth with my hand. "Is it that bad?"

She shook her head. "You're a bit pink, which is better than the sheet white you were. Give it a few and you'll be back to normal. Well, except for the whole pregnant thing." She leaned in closer, waiting for more information.

I glanced around, searching for Marjorie's nosy bat ears and any other snoopers before shuffling closer. "I found out on Wednesday. My period was way overdue, but I thought it was just stress."

"Why that?"

"It happens. I'm under a lot of pressure and sometimes that makes my period skip. I'd felt a little off, but once again, brushed it off as stress. On Wednesday I threw up, and that's when I began to think things weren't just stress related. After work I took a pregnancy test, and it was positive."

"No wonder you've been spacey all week. Why didn't you tell me, dork?"

I shook my head. "It's just been so busy." She nodded in understanding, knowing I'd worked well past the time everyone else had left the last few days and weeks. "I planned to tell you tomorrow so we could have time and privacy. Plus, I've just been trying to come to grips with it all. Trying to not completely lose my shit. Finding Richard helps."

"Well, if he'd have called you…" she trailed off, wanting me to take her bait on the topic.

"He did, and I can't be upset about it. He transposed two numbers."

Her ruffled feathers relaxed. "Well, that sucks. What now?"

"We're going to dinner and I'm so sorry, but I'm going to have to cancel tomorrow."

"You're already canceling? I mean, I'm not mad, I get it, but even before dinner you think he's going to stay?"

I nodded. I knew in my core that he wasn't leaving until he absolutely had to. "More importantly, what am I going to wear?"

She hummed and tapped on her lips. "Brent and I are going to *Maggiano's*, but I'll come over to help. We can get ready together."

"And you'll curl my hair?"

She rolled her eyes. "And I'll curl your hair."

Chapter TWO

Hours later I was fresh out of the shower and staring down at the two dresses I'd picked out. One was the standard little black dress, the other was *that* dress, the silver one I'd worn the night we met.

Was it cliché? Stupid? Was I being an idiot for even considering it?

"Knock knock!" Jenna called out as she entered, the sound of the lock clicking back into place.

"Bedroom," I called back.

She walked in with her makeup kit in one hand and her curling iron in the other. She set it all down on the bathroom vanity before coming to stand next to me.

"What do I do?"

"Oh, hell, yes," Jenna said when her gaze hit the dress I'd worn on New Year's Eve. She picked it up and brushed the other one to the side, barely looking at it. Not that she hadn't seen it before—I'd worn it to the office Christmas party.

"Not too much?"

She shook her head. "Totally fitting, but it reminds me…I can't believe you got pregnant on New Year's Eve!"

A chuckle left me. "I still can't believe you hooked up with Brent. One second you were dancing with Keenan, the next you're all over Brent."

"You were getting frisky upstairs with the man. It was a party, and Brent was there to dance. Keenan found a girl of his own. Plus, Brent is stupid tall and he can man handle my body in the best ways." Her eyes glazed over, a lopsided grin completing the dazed look.

"Almost everyone is stupid taller than us," I reminded her. There was only an inch separating us, and we were both at the bottom barrel of five feet.

"And just think how Richard is going to throw you around. You said he's jacked."

I froze, my mouth dropping open. "He picked me up and pinned me to the wall like it was nothing." My body lit up at the memory and the implications of what the night could provide.

"That's what I'm talking about!"

"But this is our first official date. At least I think it is. What if I'm reading too much into tonight? What if he just wants to talk about the baby?" I asked, worry washing over me. When was the last time I'd been so nervous over a first date?

She rolled her eyes and sat me down. "If he wanted to do that, he'd just come over and you'd order in. The man is getting reservations on the biggest date night of the year. He's doing the whole wooing thing. That tells me he wants more than sex or to talk about the bun in your oven. Though with the way you two were getting down that night, I have a feeling you'll still end up rocking it between the sheets."

"With the way we kissed in the conference room? That's a pretty safe bet." The memory alone sent a wave of heat through me.

"In no time you'll be in love, with a cute little baby bump and fighting over names."

The picture she painted made my chest clench. In the days since I learned I was pregnant, an overwhelming feeling of *oh, shit* had prevailed, and I couldn't think about anything else. I figured Jenna could help me over the weekend, but then there he was, and that spark was still there, a burning ember that burst into a scorching inferno the moment we touched.

It took a half hour for Jenna to do my hair before she disappeared to finish getting ready for her own date night. Her makeup and hair were flawless as always, and I had been with her the previous weekend when she bought a little red dress that she swore seemed modest but would allow Brent a little peep show from above.

Once she was gone, the nerves kicked in. My stomach fluttered with butterflies. I was in the middle of questioning my dress decision again when the doorbell rang. I picked up my clutch and coat on my way to the door. My heartbeat picked up with each step and my hands began to shake as my nerves revved into overdrive.

I blew out a breath before twisting the handle and pulling the door open.

Richard stood on my front stoop looking stunningly handsome. He was wearing a different suit than earlier and I was very excited to find out what was underneath.

The corner of his mouth drew up before exploding into a full-blown smile. "Very nice."

"You think?" I asked before looking down at the silver fabric. "I figured we never got to finish that night."

He nodded as he stepped forward. Once he was in range, his arm slipped around my waist and he tugged me to him.

"You got the rest of the stain out," he said as he trailed his fingers over my chest, dipping between my breasts with one finger.

"Yes," I said, noticing how low my voice had become. No matter the situation, once again, in seconds, sexual tension exploded between us.

The inches that separated us disappeared. Goosebumps erupted on my skin, his fingers trailing across my collarbone. His thumb brushed against my neck before hooking my jaw and tilting my head back. The breath tumbling from my lips became staggered and I reached up, my palm resting against his chest.

"You have no idea how much I've dreamt about this dress. Especially the view of it on my floor."

"What about me?"

His lips ghosted mine. "I think it's pretty obvious how much I've dreamt of you. In the dress. Out of the dress. Looking up at you from between your thighs." I drew in a sharp breath when he nipped at my jaw. "How fucking good it felt inside you."

I clenched my fingers, gathering the fabric of his jacket. All the weeks, the unnecessary heartache, and it felt like none of it had happened. Like we were right back in that crowded hall, lost in our own little bubble.

"Get a room!" a voice yelled from the parking lot, startling us both.

My head snapped to find Jenna hanging out the passenger window of a car, Brent behind the steering wheel, his palm popping the horn as they pulled up to wait for us to say hello.

Richard cleared his throat and stepped back so that I could pass through, making sure to lock the door.

"Jenna," Richard said with a wave.

I swore I could see a rosy color spread on his cheeks as he laughed at her.

I pulled my coat on, then slipped my hand in Richard's and we headed down the sidewalk to Brent's car.

"Have fun, you two," I said as I kissed her cheek.

"You too, babe. Keep in touch. If I don't hear from you by Sunday night, I'm coming over."

"You better bring food." I had a feeling I would need it.

"Breakfast for dinner?" she asked.

I nodded. "Perfect."

With that, they headed off and we walked to the only car in the parking lot with Illinois license plates—a black Acura RDX.

"Breakfast for dinner?" he asked as he held the door open for me.

"It's just this silly Sunday ritual we do," I explained.

He chuckled before shutting the door.

I drew in a breath, trying hard to control the crazy-person smile I could feel plastered on my face. He was everything I remembered.

Chapter THREE

Richard

The entire way to the restaurant I couldn't help but constantly glance over at her. In *that* dress, it was like we were picking right back up, like the last six weeks hadn't even passed.

Six weeks that I pined for her thinking she'd blown me off, but it was my own stupidity. I thanked that little voice that told me not to delete the contact, because that was my only saving grace. That evidence took her from standoffish to melting in my arms.

And now she was sitting in my car in *that* motherfucking dress. The one I'd clumsily spilled her drink on, then promptly shoved my hand down.

It was possibly the most idiotic move I'd ever made, but also the best.

Still, that dress did things to me. It represented weeks of fantasies, and was a reminder of how I had felt that night. How much I loved that night. How captivated I was.

"Have I told you how much I love that dress?"

Her lips pulled up into that blinding smile, making her light brown eyes sparkle. "I chose wisely. I did notice you checking me out. Repeatedly."

"Is there a problem with that?"

She gave a little hum, then winked at me. Fucking winked. All I wanted to do was stop, pull her onto my lap, and continue where we left off just after midnight.

Did we have to go to dinner?

Yes, asshole, you do. There are things to talk about. Like this whole baby business.

Baby.

It was my fault. I couldn't stop in time. I didn't want to. All of my strength went to pulling out of her, but it wasn't fast enough.

Drunk on my need for her, I had irrevocably altered our futures. The only bad thing was that it was a fluke that I found her again. Not knowing I had a child was a sickening thought, especially one with my very own Cinderella.

When driving down on Thursday for an all-day meeting on Friday, the idea of possibly running into her sat in the back of my mind, but in a city of over one million I didn't have high hopes. Still, I couldn't stop myself from staring at every face, searching her out.

I never expected her to work for the same company, to be a subordinate.

Her eyes widened when we pulled into the parking lot of *Eddie Merlot's*.

"How did you get a reservation here?"

"I sold my soul to the devil," I answered with a smirk as I found a parking spot near the back.

"Seriously."

I grinned at her. "I have my ways." *Thank you, Keenan!* He may not play football anymore, but he still had some favors, and he used one with the manager for me.

I exited the car and ran around to open her door. She took my hand, but her eyes were narrowed on me, a smirk playing on her lips. "You're not going to tell me?"

"A man has to keep some of his secrets."

The interior was as crowded as the parking lot, but thankfully the area around the hostess stand only held a few couples waiting to be seated.

"Hmm, maybe I should have worn the black dress," she said as she glanced around.

"No."

"No?"

I shook my head. "Hell, no."

I gave the hostess my name, and another appeared around the podium with menus in hand to lead us through the overcrowded space. We weaved through the throng of tables and people, coats and waiters, until we arrived at a square corner table. A tent card with the word *Reserved* sat on the red tablecloth, along with a glass vase that held a single red rose.

Nice touch, Keenan. I'd have to thank him for that later.

The wide-eyed awe on her face was worth every favor I probably owed him now.

I helped her out of her coat and pulled the chair out for her before removing my own coat. Instead of sitting across from her, I chose the seat on the same corner to be closer.

"Okay, I think I have it," she said. I quirked a brow and waited. "You already had this reservation to bring some girl who was not me, because you knew you would be here for Valentine's Day."

"What happened to the other girl?" I asked, poking holes in her illogical guess.

"You dumped her or canceled, saying you couldn't make it because of work."

I'd almost forgotten how inquisitive she was. "Interesting theory, and totally plausible, but no. And here I thought you could read me better."

She pursed her lips, and I had to stop myself from leaning over and nipping at her succulent bottom lip.

"It's the situation. The busiest restaurant night of the year, and you were able to snag a reserved table?" She narrowed her gaze at me again. "What don't I know?"

Her unrelenting questions were something I remembered from that first night. And I had to admit, I liked that aspect of her personality.

"There is a lot you don't know, just as there is a lot I don't know about you."

"Good evening," the waiter said, silencing us. "How are you two doing this evening?"

"Great. You?" Natasha asked, her attention on the man in front of us. I could tell it wasn't some flippant playback response. It was more than just politeness, and the smile that formed on his face let me know he appreciated it.

"Excellent. What can I get you to drink tonight?"

"A glass of Merlot," she said, then froze. "Wait, I'm sorry. Can I get a Sprite?"

"No problem. And for you?" He looked to me, but I was stuck staring at her. Before her order, I still couldn't believe it was real, that maybe I'd misunderstood, but changing her drink confirmed it. Solidified it.

"Bourbon. Neat." I finally got out.

She blew out a breath when he left. "I really wanted that glass of wine. I need it."

"You really are pregnant," I said in awe. I was going to be a father.

She nodded. "Trust me, I've been wrestling with that little bit of information for days."

"When did you find out?" I asked as I opened up the menu. It was a way to disguise my nervousness about the topic.

How long had she known? What had she gone through thinking she'd never find me? We never even exchanged last names that night because we thought there would be more time, and I felt terrible she found out alone.

"Wednesday."

Forty-eight hours. Not too much damage done, but I counted my lucky stars fate brought us back together.

I would process my new title later, but now I needed more of her. "I guess it's time for a crash course of getting to know you."

"Twenty questions?" she asked, folding the menu and placing it down in front of her.

"Yes."

She pursed her lips again, and again I had to restrain myself from leaning in. It seemed that was a quirk of hers when she was thinking, a mannerism I filed away.

"Ever been married?"

Right to the heart of things. The woman I met that night always went straight in, and that hadn't changed.

The waiter returned with our drinks, and I took a large sip before replying. "Yes. Divorced for seven years now."

"What happened?" she asked.

My leg began to bounce. Flashes of memories popped up, betrayal flaring in my chest. "Married young, right out of undergrad. Just didn't work out in the end. Divorced by twenty-nine and married to my job ever since."

She quirked a brow at me. "Don't hold back."

"What?"

"Why did you get divorced?"

I studied her, trying to find out if there was a way I could get out of answering, though I already knew the answer. She'd read me, knew there was more I wasn't telling her. "You'll beat everything out of me, won't you?"

She shrugged and smiled. "I did that night, did you think that would change?"

I shook my head. "No, but some things aren't easy for me to talk about."

"It was messy, then?"

My reluctance only brought more probing. She was going to dig it out of me, and while not normally first-date conversation material, the baby growing inside her was proof of a future between us no matter what happened.

Just rip it off, Rick.

"I loved her, and she smiled and kissed me and told me how much she loved me while she was having an affair with my best friend. For years."

Her mouth popped open. "Oh, Richard." She reached out and placed her hand on mine. "That's terrible."

The scars ran deep, and I swallowed as I sat back, my hand slipping from under hers. I hated talking about them, and all it made me want to do was get the fuck away from the conversation.

She reached forward and took my hand again. "Don't."

I blew out a breath and leaned forward. "I'm sorry. I'm not good at emotions." Not the deep kind at least, the kind that bared my soul.

"And so you shut down?"

Is that what I'd done? "Call it a defense mechanism."

She linked her fingers with mine so that I couldn't get away. "You don't have to defend yourself from me."

I furrowed my brow. She was the most dangerous person in the world to me. "Don't I? You woke something up inside me, something deep, and then I couldn't find you. You think I was a tyrant in that office today? Imagine my office for the last month."

"So, I made an impression?"

An impression?

I stared at her. An impression was a mild descriptor of the chaos I'd felt since meeting her. I shook my head. "No."

Her eyes tightened, and she began to turn from me but I stopped her. I cupped her face, my thumb running against her bottom lip.

"You were a full-blown collision," I said with as much conviction as I could convey. She was so much more than a mere impression. "And I'm still reeling from the aftershocks. Nothing in my life has been right since that night, Natasha."

She drew in a ragged breath, the wetness clearing from her eyes. She held up her glass. "Here's to new beginnings."

I smiled and picked up my own drink. "New beginnings." I tapped my glass to hers and we both took a sip. "Next question."

There was that purse of the lips again, and I couldn't help but lift her hand to my lips and place a kiss to her knuckles.

She watched with rapt attention, her bottom lip now secure between her teeth.

"So?"

She blinked and cleared her throat. "I feel like we have this May-December thing going on. How old are you?"

May-December? What was that? "What do you mean?"

"You're high up the corporate ladder, and you didn't just suddenly get the position. I mean, I've been at it for five years and I just made it to supervisor level."

I chuckled and nodded in understanding. "Thirty-six."

"Just growing into your sexiness. Nice." She winked at me, which made me chuckle.

The waiter interrupted us then for our order, and I was enraptured watching her interact with him. She was so personable and charming, and somehow I knew she didn't think that of herself, despite the confidence I'd seen.

When he got to me, I hadn't even really looked at what was available, but the steak and lobster was always a good answer.

"How much am I robbing the cradle?" I asked once he was gone again. The calculation my brain had already done based on the limited information I had pegged her at close to thirty, but not quite. She had a youthfulness about her, but that could have also simply been her personality.

"Not as much as that crease in your forehead thinks." She reached up and smoothed out the space between my eyes with her thumb. "I'm twenty-eight."

I took hold of her wrist, keeping it close as I leaned into my palm. "See? Perfect." I pressed my lips to the inside of her wrist.

"Any siblings, Mr. Perfect?"

"Younger sister. You?"

"Two testosterone-filled pains in my ass. One older, one younger."

I chuckled at her description of her brothers. "Which is the one that plays baseball?"

She blinked at me. "You remembered."

"I'm not sure there's anything I've forgotten about that night. With the exception of the correct order of the last four digits of your phone number."

"Younger brother. Why finance?" She rolled right into the next question.

"Because football was out and business is king," I replied without pause. "Same question to you."

"I love order in numbers."

"But you have managerial aspirations?" I asked. She was a supervisor, so there was more to it than just numbers.

"I also love to problem solve."

"Do you have Excel spreadsheets that you use in your daily life?" I asked.

Pink filled her cheeks and she stared at me wide-eyed. *Bingo.*

"It's my turn," she said, trying to divert the attention away from herself.

It was my first time seeing her with what she clearly perceived as a fault. To me, though, it was far from that, just another quirk that drew me in more.

"You do, don't you?" I asked, taking her hand and pulling her closer. She resisted, the embarrassment flooding her face despite her attempts to hide it from me. "Tell me."

"Okay! Yes, I have one for all my bills, one for my savings, one for progressive monetary investments," she rattled off, her expression set in a bit of defiance, daring me to say anything.

"Progressive monetary investments?" That one had me. She was simply too perfect if she was using that as a descriptor for her personal finances.

She let out a huff. "A fancy way of saying forecasting based on my current rate of savings."

"I'm in awe of you."

"Stop."

"Seriously. You amaze me." I placed a light kiss to her fingers, her eyes glued to mine. "You mentioned wanting to buy a condo on the river."

"Right! And it helps with that. I really want to put twenty percent down, and it shows me how much I need to save each month to attain it."

I loved the way she became animated when talking about her spreadsheets and saving money. It was adorable and appealed to my own spreadsheet-obsessed side.

"How close are you?"

She glanced down. "Well, things have changed and I haven't gotten to reevaluate my finances yet. I may have to put it off another year until after…"

She blew out a breath and swallowed as she looked around the room. A baby changed a lot and was a huge financial responsibility.

"You won't be doing it on your own," I said, drawing her attention. "No matter what happens between you and me, I will be there to help."

The uncertainty I saw in her flew away and she smiled at me. "Why Annex? Football to streaming content?"

It was an odd switch from sports to one of the top streaming content providers, up there with Netflix and Hulu, but that was how things fell.

A chuckle left me. "After my MBA I was a financial advisor for a while, then I was offered a position with one of my clients. Michael headhunted me away after my divorce, and the rest is, as they say, history."

"Michael Stanton? The president of Annex?"

I nodded. "The very same."

She seemed in awe. "I've never met him."

"Not surprising. He has a bed in his office, and a bathroom with a shower. I'm not sure he goes home often. I may be married to the job, but he practically lives in it." And that was why he was three times divorced by forty-five. Wife four was only around for the money.

Her mouth turned down. "That's kind of sad."

"How so?" I asked.

"If all you have is work…it must be lonely."

I blinked at her, trying not to show how her observation was like a knife in the chest. Being with her only highlighted how much I'd alienated myself from even the possibility of a relationship before.

Chapter
FOUR

Richard

DINNER PROGRESSED, AND I'D NEVER FELT THE LEVEL OF connection that I felt with her.

We were poking at a piece of chocolate cake when her phone went off with a text message.

"Going to check it?"

She shook her head. "No. I just want to be here with you."

It went off again. "Might be important."

She blew out a breath and pulled the phone from her clutch. Her brow scrunched as she looked at the screen.

"Well, the thought that maybe this was you is now blown out of the water."

"What?"

She shook her head. "I've gotten a couple of random text messages from an unknown number."

"Well, we know it wasn't me." I held out my hand and she set the phone on my palm.

After a couple of cursory, nondescript texts there were two new ones.

Why haven't you responded?

It's Valentine's Day. You're breaking my heart, baby.

"Given your numbers to any strange men lately?" I asked with a chuckle.

"Well, there was this one, he turned out to be mostly harmless, but hot as hell," she teased with a saucy little smirk.

A groan left me. "That dress…"

She continued on. "I mean, it was a totally inappropriate meeting. He threw liquid all over me, then dragged me into a bathroom and shoved his hand between my breasts."

I hung my head, my eyes squeezed tight as I shook my head. "That will not go down in history as one of my finer moments."

She shrugged. "You did get the stain out, and it's one hell of a story."

"You really should have at least slapped me."

"That look of absolute concentration on your face stopped me. You had no realization of what you'd done. Focused on the task."

I wanted to make an inappropriate comment about how I'd like to be focused on another task right now, like the space between her thighs, but I kept that one to myself. Instead, my fingers flew across the screen.

"What are you doing?"

"Responding," I said. Once finished, I handed the phone back.

Stop texting my girlfriend. She's not your baby, she's mine.

That bottom lip of hers ended up between her teeth again, forming a smile as she read and reread. "That should stop it. Thank you."

I grinned at her. "You're welcome."

We headed out, back to the car, to her apartment. Her hand warmed mine for the entire ride and a sense of calm washed through me.

My intent was to drop her off and go back to my hotel to pine for her. To be a gentleman and not the lust-fueled mess I was that night, and the one my senses were begging me to be again.

After helping her from the car, we walked up to her door as if we were returning from our first date, which technically we were. As we stood there I pulled her close and leaned down, pressing my lips to hers.

A simple kiss. A slow kiss.

One that promptly became hotter and deeper until I was practically holding her in the air. Little mewls of pleasure left her, and I pulled her tighter to me.

When we pulled back, we were both breathing heavily, and I didn't want to let her go.

"We never finished our night together. Would you like to come in?"

"Yes." There was no other answer.

I hated releasing her so that she could unlock the door. As soon as we were through the door, I locked it.

"Do you have condoms?" I asked, my hands on her hips, pulling her back to my chest.

"Don't need them," she said as she tossed her clutch on a nearby entry table.

"No?"

"I can't get any more pregnant," she giggled.

"STIs?"

"Got that checked after our little adventure, and got a clean bill of health. You?"

"Same. Clean."

"Now that's over, you're too far away," she said in a breathy moan as she placed her hand over the hard line of my cock. "And I didn't get a proper hello from this guy last time."

I slipped my hand between her thighs, earning a gasp of surprise, and pressed my fingers against her clit. "Ditto."

I didn't just want inside her. We did that. I wanted to taste every inch of her, devour her like a starving man. She reached down and grabbed the hem of her dress.

"Don't," I said, stopping her from pulling it over her head. "Six weeks of fantasizing about you in this dress. I'm going to be the one to take it off you."

Her tongue peeked out to wet her lips, and she relaxed her hands down to her sides.

I kept my eyes on hers as I wrapped my arms around her, noting just how tiny she really was, which only aroused me more. The way her chest heaved as I slowly slid the zipper down only amped up the reality of the moment, one I'd been dreaming about.

The weight of the dress shifted, exposing the tops of her breasts. I leaned down and nipped at one soft mound. The top slipped down more and a groan left me when her perfectly pink, pert nipples popped out.

My arms flexed, pulling her closer as my tongue flattened out to capture her nipple. She drew in a sharp breath, her hands grasping at my shoulders. Tiny whimpers left her as I sucked and licked, then nipped before making my way back up her neck to her lips.

"You are perfection, and I haven't even fully unwrapped you."

"What are you waiting for?" she asked.

"I don't want to rush it." I fell down to my knees and slowly tugged the fabric until it passed her hips. Gravity took it to the floor, but I was enraptured by the curves of her body. Curves that drew me to lean in and nip at her hip, my hands slipping under her panties. A quick tug made her cry out, her hands reaching out to steady herself on my shoulders.

A groan left me as I stared at her pretty little pussy while I blindly lifted her leg out of her panties, but I didn't put it back down. I hooked her leg over my shoulder and shifted her hips, my thumb brushing against her clit.

She drew in a sharp breath, her hips rocking ever so slightly against me.

"Something you want?" I teased, loving how turned on and desperate she'd become.

"You know what I want."

"Do I?"

She nodded. "Make me come."

A growl left me and I nipped at her inner thigh. Fuck, how I wanted to devour her. "Is that all?"

She fisted my hair, pulling me closer to what she wanted. "And fuck me until I can't walk."

I could oblige that, and leaned forward to swipe my tongue up her slit. A groan moved through me at the first taste of her and I dug in for more. She was all sweet and musk and that only drove me deeper, taking in every drop, drowning in her little mewls.

I loved the screams that came from her when I sucked hard on her clit. She grabbed my hair hard, but I didn't relent.

Her legs began shaking so hard she was unable to hold herself up, so I handled the brunt of her weight as her orgasm crashed down on her. Convulsions rocked through her, head back as she cried out.

I slowed down, gently lapping against her sensitive flesh before kissing her thigh and removing it from my shoulder. She slid down the wall until she came to a stop on my thighs.

"Okay, you were not exaggerating your skills," she said as she wrapped her arms lazily around my shoulders.

I chuckled against her neck. "All you asked was if I can make a woman come."

"I wasn't expecting it to be that good, though." Her arms fell between us and I moaned against her skin, my teeth lightly digging into her neck as she palmed my cock through my pants.

Heat raced through me and a groan crawled through my chest.

"Where do you want to come?" she whispered.

"Inside you."

I grabbed her ass, holding her close as I stood, moving into her apartment until I found her bedroom. Setting her down on the bed, I started to unbutton my shirt, while she removed her shoes, then she greedily ripped at my belt and slacks.

"Too many clothes."

A chuckle left me. She was just as desperate as I was. Within seconds she had my pants on the ground and was pushing down my boxer briefs. My dick sprang free, nearly smacking her in the face.

Her mouth popped open as she stared, then blinked at it. I pulled my undershirt off and threw it on the ground, then toed off my shoes to step out of my pants.

"Fuck," she hissed.

"What?"

She shook her head. "I mean, it's no wonder I ended up pregnant. I think I just got pregnant again from looking at it."

That stroked my ego, and it gave a twitch.

I barely blinked before her mouth was suddenly around the head.

"Shit!" I cried out at the sudden surge of pleasure that rocketed through me. I watched as her lips stretched around, her tongue swirling around the tip.

A few more bobs of her head and I gently pulled her off. "I guess I should have specified. I want to come inside your pussy." I leaned over her until she was forced to lay back and crawl farther up onto the bed. "Deep inside."

She took my face in her hands and drew me down to her lips as I settled between her thighs. There was no more teasing, no more waiting. I rubbed the head between her folds, then pressed forward.

Fuck! My vision went white at the explosion of sensory overload.

I'd forgotten how good it felt to be bare inside a woman. Warm and snug and hitting every nerve. Each stroke fueled the next. I didn't care about the burn in my muscles, only about the pleasure of her wrapped around me as I drove us both to the height of pleasure.

I couldn't take my eyes off her face—the absolute personification of lust.

Our eyes were locked. With each thrust, each keen of pleasure from her lips, her perfection increased.

I slammed my hips into hers, faster, as my balls drew up. Each hit deep inside had her crying out. Her nails dug into my skin, her body tensing. She was coming again and I willed myself to hold back, never deviating from the force of my thrust.

She broke, and her already tight pussy began milking my cock. I couldn't hold back anymore, and slammed into her. With a growl I erupted. Deep, satiating, and core-deep completeness washed through me.

We were both shaking, and strength left me. I dropped down to my forearms as I tried to regain my breath.

"Can we do that again?" she asked as her fingers lazily drew circles on my arm.

I smiled and nodded against her shoulder. "Hell, yes."

Chapter
FIVE

Natasha

We never left my apartment on Saturday, with the exception of running to Richard's hotel to gather his clothes, check him out, and pick up some food on our way back. We barely wore clothes. The entire time we were together, we were either eating or having sex.

There were also downtimes where we just lay there and talked.

"Seriously, though, I don't understand why they didn't get an interim for Nina," Richard said. We were recovering from our third round of the day, lying in bed and just talking. It felt so good to have that as well as the physical. Conversation wasn't filled with all fluff thanks to our mutual employer.

"Because there was no one. Trent getting fired created a hole and luckily I was chosen to fill it, but it takes an average of six months to fully understand a position, and I wasn't in it three weeks before Nina was rushed to the hospital."

"Is she okay?" he asked. I wondered if he even knew before the meeting that she was out.

I nodded. "She's doing well, the baby too, but she's on bed rest."

"When is the baby due?"

"Around the first of April."

He nodded, and I had a feeling he was doing some sort of calculation in his head. "And when is our baby due?"

In all our conversations over the past few days, we'd barely mentioned the elephant in the room. A little at dinner, but since then it had been all about us. "September twenty-third."

He nodded, but his attention drifted.

I reached out and brushed his hair from his forehead. "What are you thinking about?"

"Just a few months ago I was home alone having one too many drinks and lamenting my life. Thirty-six with no romantic life, a bad divorce, and no children, and I wondered if that would ever change or if I would spend the rest of my life in this lonely prison I've created." He rolled me over onto my back and slipped down between my legs, his eyes glued to my abdomen. "I wasn't sure I'd ever be a father." He gently caressed the skin before placing a soft kiss there. "Thank you."

"For telling you to just pull out?" I asked.

He nipped at my hip bone. "Smartass."

I shrugged.

He trailed his lips from hip to hip, his stubble tickling my skin. "Thank you for making me a father. We barely know each other, but I've never felt this way before."

"I thought you didn't like to talk about your emotions?" Or was it just some emotions?

"Some are easier than others."

I ran my hand down his shoulder to his elbow. "I've never felt this way either," I admitted. It was true. Whatever we had, whatever drew us together, was overpowering. Impossible to deny. "How are we going to make this work?"

"It helps to have the right number. And it's just under a four-hour drive. We can easily spend the weekends together."

"But then what?" The million-dollar question.

He was quiet for a moment. "What's your favorite color?" He

asked as he moved to lay next to me again, propping his head on his elbow.

"Are you trying to distract me from my question? Because it's not going to work."

He chuckled. "No, but before we get ahead of ourselves, let's start with the basics. We never finished our game the other night. My favorite color is orange."

I hmmed as I thought about it, about my happy place. Jenna and I had gone on vacation to the Bahamas two years prior. It was the most relaxed I'd been in years.

"The color of the water in the Bahamas. Swinging in a warm breeze, sipping on a fruity drink, the sun warming my skin, the sand, and the sound of the waves."

"That's quite a color," he said.

"Sorry, it just reminded me of the reasons why it's my favorite."

His fingertips danced across my skin, leaving the burn of a dying fire in their wake. "Maybe one day you can show me."

Warmth blossomed in my chest. He may not have been good with expressing deeper emotions, but happiness was one that exuded from him. It was uninhibited and flowed from him with ease and without pretense. They weren't empty words and false promises, but honest wishes, and I wished with him.

I turned into him and pushed him onto his back, my head above his heart.

"I hate that you have to go back," I said as my fingers traced lazy circles on his chest.

"Me too." He blew out a breath and bent his neck to place a kiss to the crown of my head. "I needed this. God, did I need this."

I propped my head up on his arm. "I hope this means I have more time to get done what Mr. Bennett wanted."

He chuckled. "On paper, no, but I think I can extend the deadline by a few days." Leaning forward, he pressed his lips to mine. "I'm sorry everything was thrown on you all at once. It was unfair for you to be thrown into the lion's den like that."

I continued my caressing, and lightly tipped my nails into his skin. "That lion has sharp teeth."

He hummed. "Just keep petting him and you'll tame him."

I bit down on my bottom lip trying to contain my foolish grin while I continued to run my fingers across his skin.

"Have you been to the doctor yet?" he asked a few hours later as we sat on the floor eating lunch at my coffee table. "I mean, I know you've only known for a few days."

The pregnancy was a topic we'd mostly avoided, and with good reason. We'd missed out on the rest of that night, and we spent two days making up for that lost time. But out of sight, out of mind didn't deter the fact that there was a baby with us. One that couldn't be seen or felt, but was there nonetheless.

"No. I have an appointment on Thursday afternoon."

His shoulders slumped. "I can't make it."

Reaching across the coffee table, I took his hand in mine, linking our fingers together.

"It's okay."

His lips formed a thin line. "Not really."

"Yes, really," I assured him before taking a sip of tea. "I want you there, but the reality is we live over three hours apart. Doctor's appointments are going to be during the week. That's the nature of them."

His eyes met mine. "I want to be there."

The conviction in his eyes made my chest clench. "I'll try to make late afternoon appointments. Maybe on Fridays?"

He nodded in agreement. "That might work." He blew out a breath. "This is all so weird."

"You're telling me," I scoffed. "The last thing I expected from that night was this."

Under the table he hooked my calf and stroked the inside of my knee with his thumb. "I know we're not exactly strangers like we were Friday night, but I need you to know I'm hooked on you. I want a relationship with you. I have since the moment I met you."

I pulled his hand forward and nipped at his knuckle. "Maybe I'll make you less married to your job."

His lip twitched up. "Maybe. I know we have a lot to discuss about our baby, but I'm not sure we're at a place to do that right now."

I nodded in agreement, staring down at my mug, at the little flecks of escaped tea leaf bits at the bottom. "Honestly, I'm still in panic mode. I haven't even begun to think of what changes this means."

"We are agreed, then, that it can wait a little while, until we've been together longer, to figure it out?"

I reached up and threaded my fingers with his. "Definitely. More time to process. Figuring out how I'm going to explain this situation to my parents."

He straightened a bit at that. "I've been so caught in our little bubble I didn't even think about other people knowing."

I let out a sigh. "I know this is completely unexpected, but we can take our time. September is still seven months away."

"When did you plan to tell your parents?" he asked.

"My brothers both live here, so I guess it depends on Wyatt's schedule."

He scrunched his brow. "Wyatt?"

"My little brother. He's the baseball player."

He nodded. "How many brothers again?"

While I'd mentioned the two heathens, I hadn't gone much into depth besides telling him one was a baseball player. "One more—Carson. He's two years older than me."

He contemplated my brother situation. "So one experienced bat handler and an older brother to contend with."

"What does that mean?" I asked, trying not to laugh at his description.

He shrugged. "I'm just wondering if I should wear some sort of body armor."

I rolled my eyes and giggled. "They'll give you shit, but you'll be fine. Now, if you fuck with me, I don't know how they'll respond to that."

"Don't fuck with you. Check. Can I still fuck with you when we're alone?" he asked as he nipped at my knuckle.

"You aren't spent yet?"

His lip pulled up into a sexy little smirk. "Six weeks of buildup does not go away that fast."

I glanced at the clock. It was already late in the afternoon. "Hmm, one more time before you go?"

He scooted around to my side of the table. "Wasn't there an ultimatum?" His lips ghosted mine. I drew in a breath, my body lighting up at his closeness. "To leave you sorely aching?"

I grabbed onto his arm as he manhandled me onto his lap. "There was."

"Are you there yet?"

"Not yet."

He pushed the table away and turned me onto my back, pinning me to the ground, caging me in his arms. I drew in a sharp breath.

"Then my work here isn't finished."

Just then, my neighbors, who had been unusually quiet, started slamming against the wall. Richard's eyes widened at the moans and screams coming from the other side of the drywall. Another hard slam, and the pictures hanging on our shared wall jostled.

"Holy shit, you're right. Your neighbors do scream a lot."

"I told you."

His eyes met mine and that sexy grin turned wicked. "You know what this makes me want to do, right?"

I gave him my best side eye, because that smirk he was flashing was going to set me on fire.

"What?"

"Just a little competition between neighbors. See who can scream the loudest."

"You're all about the competition, aren't you?"

He shrugged and wet his lips with his tongue, which only hastened my descent into his erotic madness.

"Plus it's an opportunity to really show you how you affect me by fucking you straight through the wall."

Chapter SIX

Natasha

DAYS LATER I WAS BEYOND EXHAUSTED.

Richard made good on his promise, and when he left hours later, I could barely move from my bed. Jenna came over and promptly turned around, telling me I had to clean my "sex den" before she'd come in. At least she left the food.

Since then I'd worked twelve-hour days trying to meet VP Bennett's expectations. While he'd given me leeway with time, I wanted to hit his original date. That way when things came out, it wouldn't seem like he was giving me special treatment.

Though the rumor mill was already running thanks to Jenna's little outburst, so far most of it was nothing more than the fact that I got pregnant on New Year's. Richard's name was left out, but I had a feeling that little fact was running through the half dozen others from management that were in the meeting.

After a long day I was finally walking into my apartment, ready to fall asleep, when my phone went off.

Thank you for not making me be an asshole to you again—Richard

You don't HAVE to be an asshole about it—Natasha

A moment later my phone went off, Richard's name flashing across the screen.

"Hi."

"Hi. Sadly that is the only way I've found for shit to get done. And as much as I want to, I can't give you special treatment," he said.

"That's also something I don't want," I agreed. I definitely didn't want anyone thinking I was fucking my way up. "I worked hard to get this position, and I don't want people thinking it's because I'm sleeping with the boss."

A groan vibrated in my ear, and I was stunned how my pussy twitched at the sound even over the phone. I switched him over to speaker so I could change my clothes, dying to get out of my office attire and into my yoga pants.

"If you were here right now I would be acting out so many fantasies," he said, his voice low with a hint of gravel that only turned me on more.

Then my brow scrunched as I thought about what he said. I stripped off my shirt and stared down at my phone. "Please tell me you aren't still at the office."

There was silence followed by a clearing of his throat. "How do you think I knew the GLs were cleaned up?"

My mouth dropped open. "Richard! It's almost nine. Go home." I pulled my pants off and threw them in the laundry, my bra following. My mouth popped open at the pain from the tenderness in my breasts.

"I'm working on it."

"Why are you still there?" I asked as I pulled my nightshirt on followed by my fuzzy socks. In the background I could hear the tick of his fingers tapping on his keyboard.

"I'm analyzing the profits for a meeting," he said, his voice monotone, indicating his level of concentration.

"Do it tomorrow," I said. He deserved a break just like every other employee, but I had a feeling he wasn't one for taking them. Which then sent me down the rabbit hole of wondering how many vacation days he'd built up. I wasn't even going to ask, because I was certain it was a level that would probably make me fall over in shock.

"The meeting is in the morning, and I have to have January included."

Oh.

It wasn't some arbitrary, throwing-his-weight-around request he'd made. He was unable to do his job completely until we had closed the month out.

"What if it had taken me longer?" I asked.

"Then I would get shit for having estimates this late in the month, and would have to send out revised documents as soon as the information was available," he said as he continued to plug away. "Can you do me a favor?"

I headed into the bathroom and removed my eye makeup—the extent of my daily cosmetics wear. "What's that?"

He sighed, the keys stopping. "Work only eight hours tomorrow." The softness in his tone had returned, and it melted me. "I'm not there to make sure you're taking care of yourself, and I know you worked long hours the last few days."

"I should have been a forensic accountant with how deep I was into all that." With a splash of water, I dabbed my face before throwing my hair into a loose bun.

"Don't redirect."

"I wasn't!" I cried out.

"Yes, you were." He chuckled. "I know you a little more each day, and that includes how you avoid topics."

"Fine," I said as I pursed my lips. "Eight hours tomorrow."

"And Friday."

"Richard," I groaned.

"You're pregnant. You need to take it a little easier."

"I will," I promised. I really wished he was there with me so I could curl up in his warmth. I missed him.

"Forty-hour work weeks," he stressed.

I moved to the kitchen and pulled open the fridge in search of something to snack on. "You do understand how hard that is, don't you?"

"Considering a light week for me is fifty, yes."

Fifty? I really hoped I had the ability to divorce him from that many hours. All jokes of him being married to his job aside, he was going to have to figure out a balance. There was still time, but the sooner he started carving out time, the better.

"How are you feeling?"

A sigh left me, and I pulled out a container of Panera mac and cheese. "Well, whoever has been heating up their breakfast every morning for the past week stopped today, so no vomiting up my breakfast."

"Not vomiting is always a good thing. What was it, so I avoid accidentally ordering or eating it when we're together?"

"Oddly it's turkey sausage, not pork. And I love turkey sausage, so that sucks." My favorite breakfast was one of those frozen breakfast sandwiches with turkey sausage. I had a full box in my fridge that I was going to have to throw out or give to Jenna.

"No turkey sausage. Check. Now, get to bed, little girl."

"Excuse me?"

"I'm talking to my little girl," he said, his tone playful. "You go take her to bed."

I rolled my eyes and laughed as I popped the container into the microwave and set the timer. "You're too much, Mr. Bennett."

"Miss Cates…I miss you."

I smiled down at the phone, at his name. "I miss you, too. Now go finish and get to bed yourself. Baby bean and I are going to eat some mac and cheese, then go finish off a pint of ice cream."

"Not exactly healthy eating."

"No, it's tired eating," I said with a chuckle. "Goodnight, Richard."

"Goodnight, Natasha," he replied softly.

The click indicated the call ended, then his name disappeared from the screen. I let out a sigh, my fingers running across the glass.

Two more days. That was all I had to wait until I saw him again.

I was a good girl and did as he requested on Thursday, and I was halfway through Friday when a deep voice pulled me from my bubble of concentration.

"Miss Cates, can I see you in the conference room?"

I jerked at the voice drawing me from my screen and the financial statement I'd been going over.

There was no stopping, no giving me an opportunity to even register the request, but it was Richard's form walking away toward the conference room. My brow scrunched as I rose from my seat and followed. I was both excited and confused by his sudden arrival. When we talked on the phone the night before, he said he would try to leave before Friday-night traffic, but it wasn't even rush hour in Indianapolis yet.

When I passed across the threshold, the door closed behind me.

Once again, there was not even a fraction of a second for me to process what was going on when strong hands pulled at me until my feet no longer touched the ground.

My legs wrapped around his waist just before my back pressed against the wall. His lips crashed to mine, frantic and demanding, and I melted into it. There was desperation in his touch and need in his rocking hips, but desire fueled his tongue against mine.

It was intoxicating as every nerve reacted—his greed was infectious, and I met him in kind.

Our teeth knocked as he changed the angle, his lips demanding, but it wasn't enough. I drew in a shuddering breath when he yanked at the buttons of my shirt and pulled my breast from the cup of my bra. My nipple tensed between his fingers, and my hips rocked against the hardness pressed against my clit.

His teeth sent tingles through me as he worked his way down my jaw to my neck where he licked at the skin.

"I need you," he whispered with a groan.

My fingers flexed against him and my back arched as he drew my breast into his mouth. Every cell begged that I throw caution to the wind and let him fuck me against the wall like we both desperately wanted. They argued that he was the VP and it didn't matter, but I knew it did.

I knew the speed with which gossip moved through the office.

"We can't," I said as I tore myself away from him. There were too many people outside the door and walls that had marginal sound insulation. Plus there were just too many clothes to remove. If I'd had any inclination he was going to come in the middle of the day, I might have worn a skirt.

He continued to paw at me, his hand between my legs rubbing against my clit. My vision blurred from the pleasure, my body begging to give him what he wanted because I wanted it too, but we couldn't where we were.

I yanked his hand from me, his clouded eyes scrunched before he reached for me again. I pulled free from his grip and dropped to my knees before he could catch me and worked open his belt and slacks. His cock was hard, begging for release. The head was almost purple and when I wrapped my lips around the tip, I was rewarded with a low groan.

His fingers lightly cupped my jaw, eyes heavy and dark as he watched me work my way down each inch.

"Fuck, my cock looks so good between your lips," he said in a low groan.

I couldn't get all of him in before my gag reflex kicked in.

"Fuck," he hissed as I gagged around him. His hips flexed, chasing his desperate need to come.

With one hand I jerked the base in time with the bobbing of my head. His groans grew louder as his hips sped up.

I glanced up and was lost in the trance-like stare of his eyes. His movement paused, pushing his hips forward, as deep into my mouth as he could go.

His cock jerked, warm cum splashing against the back of my throat. I swallowed around him, loving the sounds rumbling from his chest. His breath was heavy when with one last jerk of his cock, he pulled from between my lips.

"Well...that's quite a start to our second date," I said as I wiped at my mouth with the back of my hand.

Chapter SEVEN

Richard

When the fog of lust cleared, I realized what I shouldn't have done—mauled Natasha in the conference room. It had made perfect sense at the time, but that was the kind of shit thinking a hard dick could manage.

Still... The image of her looking up at me, mouth stuffed with my cock, was number one in my spank bank.

"Sorry," I said as I helped her from the floor.

"Feel better?" she asked. Her hair was a mess, lips puffy and pink.

"Yes."

"Good, because you owe me."

I quirked my brow at her. Tit for tat with her. "Before or after dinner?"

She bit down on her lower lip, and that was when I caught the heaviness in her eyes and the flush of her cheeks. The sight was seductive, and made me want her more.

"Or right now?"

"You're early," she said, deflecting again, though I was certain it was to steer the conversation away from sex.

"You were at forty-two hours for the week before you even came in today."

"Did you check my time?" she asked with a quirk of her brow.

"Of course," I said as I stuffed my relieved dick back in my pants, then fixed my clothes.

She rolled her eyes and stepped forward, her hands resting on my sides. "Hi."

"Hi," I said as I looped my arms around her, holding her close. The warmth of her body and the floral scent of her skin calmed me.

"What are you doing here so early?"

"I came to break you out of here," I said as I brushed her hair behind her ears in order to tame the mess I'd made.

She shook her head. "I'm not done."

"And to talk to you about a project."

She tilted her head. "A project?"

"Yes."

Voices filtered from the other side of the door, and she pulled away.

"Let's talk somewhere else," I said as I pulled the door open to find Marjorie standing just outside.

Fuck.

"Richard, I'm sorry, I didn't realize you were coming today," Marjorie said, her eyes wide. The panic of my sudden appearance was obvious, especially in the way she looked around the cubes. Probably silently praying everyone was complying with company policy—shit that I didn't really care about, though I knew someone in the company did. If they were doing their jobs, that was all that mattered to me.

"Are you my secretary?" I asked, pulling any warmth from my tone. Marjorie was a nosy busybody and I couldn't stand that behavior.

"N-no. I'm just surprised, is all," she said with a stutter.

"I have business with Miss Cates that doesn't concern you, and I will be in need of your office." God, I was such an ass sometimes.

"Of course," she said with a strained smile. "Just let me get my laptop and it's all yours."

I placed my hand on Natasha's lower back and ushered her down the hall. In reality, I gave no fucks if people knew we were together. I was the fucking VP, and didn't answer to any of them.

We waited for Marjorie to grab whatever she needed, and I tried to not even look at her so that I didn't engage her nagging need for verification.

"Let me know if you need anything," she said just as I shut the door in her face.

My jaw clenched, and I blew out a breath before taking a seat in her chair.

"Why her office?" Natasha asked as she took one of the open chairs opposite me. "Nina's office is available."

Logically, that would have been the correct move, but something about Marjorie brought on my desire to be vindictive.

"Because Marjorie is an insufferable, brown-nosing, ass-kissing, tattle-telling twatwaffle."

Natasha's brow rose. "Tell me how you really feel."

"Irritated," I growled.

"You didn't need her office, did you?"

"Nope." I clenched my teeth as I looked over her desk. Every little thing was in perfect order and in perfect compliance. "But I did need to remind her I'm her boss."

"Well, I hope when you're reminding me you're my boss, it's not by taking over my office…or cubicle as it were."

My lips twitched as I finally began to relax. "Your body, then?"

She leaned forward. "You can show me how you're the boss tonight."

My tongue snuck out to wet my lips. "I'd love to. I also need to do it here."

"I just sucked you off," she reminded me.

A chuckle left me. "Not that."

She leaned back into the chair and crossed her legs. "What can I do for you, Mr. Bennett?"

Fuck, my name from her lips. Maybe showing her I was the boss all over Marjorie's desk wasn't such a bad idea.

"Mmm, I like the way you say my name."

"Pervert."

"Perhaps." I rubbed my jaw and settled myself into the conversation I brought her in here for, and not for the sex-filled thoughts I was having. Instead, I needed to initiate the scheme that came to me on the drive. "You are Nina's interim, and that means you have the joy of budget planning."

The blood drained from her face. "Excuse me?"

Not the reaction I was expecting. "You and I are going to analyze the profits and losses from the first half of the fiscal year."

"The two of us?"

I nodded. "I have to report financial information, including the financial welfare of the business to help with decisions that will be made based on the information."

Her brow furrowed and she shook her head. "Richard, I'm barely keeping my head above water here. Six weeks ago I was a staff accountant. For three weeks I was a corporate supervisor in training, then three weeks as that and interim manager. And for the last two weeks I've tried not to be run over by the steam-roller that is the VP of Finance, which is you."

I gave her an apologetic smile. "There are some big business moves on the horizon, but only if we can show that it is fiscally possible."

While it wasn't necessarily needed, and I'd never called upon Nina for her help before, it was a way I could be close to Natasha more. Yes, it could help her having her name attached to the analysis, but it was my own selfishness to be closer to her that was driving my idea.

My heart jumped as I read her face. *She's going to turn me down.*

"I can tell you're about to turn me down, and I'm not above begging at this point," I said, stopping her because I wanted it for us, an opportunity to work together. "This budget planning will decide the next steps Annex takes. Getting all the information and analyzing everything together is a two-person job."

She pursed her lips. "Normally I would jump at the opportunity, but I'm absolutely exhausted. There's just too much on me right now, along with growing a human being that drains me more every day, and it sounds like someone directly below you is the person for the job, not me."

Every single point she made was valid, but I needed her.

"It falls on Nina's position due to her proximity to all the account details. You know all the shortcomings, which side businesses are profiting and which aren't, without even digging for an answer because your department balances the books on a daily basis. Having someone in my department do it just creates severe aggravation and one time caused the demotion of an employee."

"So, this isn't something you're doing just to see me?" she asked, seeming to buy into my flimsy logic while also confirming she saw right through me.

I nodded. "The added bonus is working with you. Bottom line is I report financial information that makes business decisions, and you are intimate with the financials of the business."

"That's a lot of departments."

"How much money does streaming membership bring in monthly?" I asked to test her out.

"Just under a billion dollars. In the last year it's been as low as seven hundred million and as high as one billion."

"And what is the running cost?"

"With the new programming, we're about six hundred and fifty million. It can fluctuate depending on what is in the works."

Right on target. While my reasoning was selfish, I truly believed she would be an asset.

"Those are numbers I know because I have to keep up on the

financial well-being of the company, but your position is possibly the only other that keeps an up-to-date tally of the profit and loss of the company." My logic was thin, and while I had called on Nina in the past when evaluating the company's finances, it wasn't something she worked on directly with me.

"What are they looking to buy that demands this kind of future broadcast and past financial numbers?" she asked.

All of her questions showed me why she'd been promoted. They also indicated her ability to level up in the company with ease.

"There are multiple answers to that, from studio spaces to in-house sound companies to upgrades to the platform and marketing strategies. It all costs money."

"What's in it for me?" she asked.

Fuck. "Recognition for a job well done. Maybe a bonus, but don't hold me to that." I'd have to talk to Michael about that. In all the years, I'd never called down for help past my own assistants, who drove me mad. They weren't trained or equipped for the task.

After a few torturous moments of deliberation, she stood and held out her hand.

I looked to her, almost in awe that my plan worked, before slipping my hand in hers.

"It'll be a pleasure working with you, Mr. Bennett."

"Excellent. I look forward to seeing what you can do."

We spent the next hour going over some of the logistics, with her taking notes on all the information I needed her to gather. Schedules were consulted, and we found it best to have weekly face-to-face meetings on Fridays and possibly more depending on how things came together.

When we emerged from Marjorie's office, she popped up like a gopher from one of the nearby empty cubicles, igniting my irritation again, but I did my best to stuff it down.

"Thank you, Marjorie," I said with a nod.

"Is there anything I can help you with, Richard?"

I quirked a brow at her. "With?"

"Well, Natasha is overwhelmed right now. I'd be happy to assist you in any way I can."

The vein in my forehead pulsed. What was it about the woman I found so insufferable I wasn't sure, but she irritated me to no end. "How do you know Natasha's current workload?"

"She's always complaining about how much she has to do. I mean, just look at the disorder of her department. There are violations everywhere and there are an above-average number of open statements," Marjorie said, a smug look of superiority lighting up her face.

Even Natasha, who I had yet to see get upset, was almost vibrating beside me.

"Marjorie, do I need to remind you that you are not my boss? That you have no idea what I do and hold no sway over my section?" Natasha said, barely holding in her annoyance. "My people are working hard and if they want two damn cups of coffee at their desk, they can have them."

I couldn't stop my lips from drawing up as Natasha put Marjorie in her place. Marjorie was not her boss, and it confused me why she would think making Natasha look bad would be favorable for her.

"Sounds like an irrelevant issue, Marjorie," I said in agreement. "It's obvious they are working hard, so this is a petty complaint on your part."

Marjorie's mouth turned down and she let out a little huff before wishing me a good day, ignoring Natasha completely.

"What's going on?" Jenna asked, appearing from the sea of cubicles as she watched Marjorie stomp off.

"Your boss is…frustrating," Natasha said through gritted teeth.

My brow rose, and I internally applauded her composure. It was a better answer than I would have released. "How restrained."

"Imagine working for the…frustrating," Jenna said, also holding back on all the bad things she probably wanted to fling from her mouth.

While I didn't believe Marjorie was a bad person or bad at her job, her personality was so grating and annoying. Over the phone it wasn't so strong, but in person it was instant. Her need to be seen and acknowledged, putting people down in order to shine, was not the kind of behavior I could stand.

Natasha slipped her hand in mine, and the tension melted away. I turned to her and she gave a shy look as she glanced around for anyone watching.

I would suffer Marjorie every week just to spend a few extra hours with Natasha.

Chapter EIGHT

Natasha

It quickly became apparent one Wednesday evening that Richard was not well versed in the world of texting with emojis. In fact, his texting was stiff and lacked a flow.

What started off as innocent had me rolling on the floor in laughter, slamming my hand on my kitchen table as I tried not to pee myself from laughing so hard.

I miss the sweetness of your lips—Richard

That was the first message that popped up onto my phone as I cooked dinner. It was sweet and made my chest clench.

I miss your warmth—Natasha, I typed back.

I miss your warmth, too. Especially the warmth between your thighs—Richard

I quirked a brow at the screen. Someone was feeling frisky.

Perv—Natasha

What can I say, my every thought is of you, including the very dirty ones—Richard

Well, now all I can think of is your 🍆 in my 🍑—Natasha

I bit my lip as I stared down at the screen, waiting for his response, but when it came I stared down at it in disbelief.

I have no idea what that means. Is that an eggplant?—Richard

Oh, my.

Lol. It's a euphemism—Natasha

For what?—Richard

Wow, he really was clueless about emoji-speak. I didn't want to spell it out because I was having too much fun with him not understanding I was talking about his dick, so I kept going.

For this week that needs to hurry up because I want you. In me. Eggplant to taco—Natasha

I can't decide if I'm turned on or if you want me to smash a taco with an eggplant—Richard

Oh, baby, yes, my 🌮 wants to be smashed by your 🍆 —Natasha

I get there are different kinks, but I never pegged you for a food fetish kind of girl—Richard

😂😂😂 I'm dying!—Natasha

💋💋💋—Natasha

The phone rang, but when I answered it all I could get out was laughter. I couldn't even form words.

"What is so funny?"

That just made the laughing worse.

"An eggplant—" my stomach clenched from my deep chuckles "—means dick."

"Shit," he cursed before joining in. "I get it now. My dick wants to be in your pussy too, but why the fuck does an eggplant mean dick?"

I wiped the tears from my eyes. "I have no idea, it's just become the universal symbol."

"Hmm. Wouldn't a hot dog or a banana be better?" he asked.

"Probably, but at some point someone decided eggplant was it."

My phone buzzed and I looked down to find a new text message.

🍆🌮🍆🌮🍆🌮💦💦—Richard

I bit down on my lower lip. He'd even found the squirting emoji.

"Mr. Bennett, oh my," I said in mock incredulity.

A groan left him. "Fuck, I wish you were here."

"What would I be doing?" I asked.

"Draining my eggplant with your tight little taco," he growled.

Oh, I liked that. "Would I be straddling you in your chair or would you swipe everything off your desk and lay me back?"

"Bend you the fuck over, smack your ass, and drill my cock into you. Pull your hair and make you fucking scream for more."

Fuck, he made me wish I could teleport to him so he could do just that.

I could hear something faint in the background, but couldn't quite make it out. "Do you have your eggplant out right now?"

"Yes," he hissed.

Fuck. He was masturbating in his office thinking of me.

"In this fantasy, where are you going to come?" I asked. My breathing had picked up in time with his and my thighs were clenching and unclenching.

"Slam my hips into you and fire off deep inside."

I loved the richness of his voice, the edge of desperation coloring the tone. He was desperate, and I was desperate to hear him get off. Then I would go play with my little pink vibe and replay the sound over and over in my head.

"You're going to fill my little pussy?"

"Fuck, yes, baby," he growled. "Every fucking time."

I bit down on my lips as I tried to think about what might send him over the edge. I made my voice higher in pitch. "But it's not a safe day, Mr. Bennett."

I was already pregnant, so it didn't matter, but by the sounds he was making, the idea of coming inside me on a fertile day excited him.

"Fucking…" he trailed off, nothing but a litany of moans littered with curse words could be heard. His breath was harsh, echoing into the phone, and it took him a moment for him to calm down enough to speak.

I already had my hand between my thighs, my middle finger pressed against my clit, ready to meet up with my vibe.

"Shit. I really want to find you one of those catholic school girl outfits now," he said once he caught his breath.

A giggle left me. "I might just happen to have a short plaid skirt in my closet. However, I'm beginning to think you have an impregnation fetish."

"Maybe, but if I do, it's all your fault," he said.

"My fault?"

"Mm-hmm. Because all I can think about is how fucking hot that night was, and what it made."

That night was hot. It was a night I would never forget, and for more reasons than the one brewing inside me.

He blew out a breath. "I should clean up this mess you made me make and finish up this email so I can head home."

A chuckle left me at his placing the blame on me. "Okay." I let out a sigh. "Friday can't come soon enough."

"Two days," he said in a low voice. "Goodnight, Natasha."

"Night, Richard."

I hung up the phone and promptly went into the bedroom and fired up my vibe.

We were week one into the budget planning project. At first I thought it was just an excuse to see me or help me with a promotion or something.

And I was fairly certain I was correct, but he'd also made a lot of good points as to why I was the only person to help. While there was no way I could replace Nina, if I showed initiative and skill, it could help me move into a different position. One that paid more.

More money was definitely on the brain. With a baby on the way, my finances were going to drastically change. Not to mention I would need more space. The plan I'd made with Jenna to move into the condos by the river was now a necessity. One that I needed to get rolling on…if I could find the energy for it.

Sadly I wouldn't have as much money to put down as I wanted to, but I couldn't stay in my small one-bedroom.

"Miss Cates," Richard's voice called, pulling me from the mess of a nest of papers on my desk.

I held my finger up to signal I needed a moment and continued my shuffling and straightening.

"You're really going to keep me waiting?" he asked.

I didn't even look up at him. "You're really going to ask me that?"

"Ah…"

I flipped through the stack until I found the page I needed, then turned to my computer to input an entry into the system. Once I'd saved it, I turned and looked up to Richard.

"Mr. Bennett, what can I help you with today?"

He raised an eyebrow. "Did you forget we have a meeting?"

I pursed my lips and turned back to my computer to raise my calendar. "Why yes, we did. At two. It's three-thirty."

The smug expression slid from his face, and changed to one of confusion before he rolled his eyes. "Fucking time zones," he hissed.

"You're in luck that I kinda forgot and have been working my ass off for the last hour and change," I said as I closed out of what I was working on.

"Am I?"

I nodded. "Yes, otherwise I wouldn't be nearly as friendly."

"Friendly, huh?"

I gave him a smile and a wink. "Conference room?"

"Read my mind."

After locking my computer, I grabbed the document folder and pulled my laptop from the docking station. No sooner did I stand than Marjorie arrived.

"Richard. How nice to see you."

"Marjorie," Richard said with a strained smile.

While I had a dislike for the woman, as did most who worked for her, Richard's level of tolerance was on the ground as he stomped on it.

"What brings you down?" she asked, that fake smile plastered on her face. Why was she always trying to brown-nose him?

"Miss Cates and I are working on budget analysis for an upcoming purchase proposition."

Marjorie's mouth pulled into a strained smile, and she aimed her dagger eyes at me. "Really? I wasn't aware."

"Of course not, because it doesn't concern you." Richard set his hand on my lower back and directed me toward the conference room.

I could still feel Marjorie's eyes on me when we entered.

"I think Marjorie has a lady boner for you," I said after the door had shut.

He let out a groan and shook his head. "Don't say that."

"Why not? She may be Miss Priss, but she's still pretty."

"It's that lording attitude I can't stand."

"Says the king of finance," I said, pointing out he was a bit of a lorder himself.

He let out a small chuckle as he wrapped his arm around my waist and pulled me closer. "I guess that makes you my queen."

"There you go trying to be all smooth."

"Are you saying my mojo isn't working?"

I pursed my lips. "Ask me when we aren't here."

He ran his hands up my back, then down to my waist. "Maybe we should skip out early to test it out."

I wrapped my arms around his shoulders. "I'll make out with you if you focus on the budget for an hour."

"With groping?" he asked with a quirk of his brow.

"Over the clothes."

"Before or after?"

"After, but I'll give you a hello stud kiss before we begin." I stood on the tips of my toes, straining to reach him.

"Shorty," he teased before leaning down to meet me.

As we sat, a burning sensation crawled up my throat and I grimaced as I rubbed my hand against my chest. "Crap."

"Everything okay?" he asked, his brow furrowed as he stared at me.

"Fine. It's just baby-induced heartburn."

His eyes widened. "The pregnancy causes it?"

I nodded. "One of the many fun things happening with my body lately," I said as I shook my head. "I've got some antacids in my desk. I'll be right back."

"Wait," he said stopping me. He dug through his computer bag and pulled out a container.

"Aren't you prepared," I said as I shook a few tablets onto my palm.

"I love green peppers, but my stomach doesn't," he explained. "I always have some nearby."

"Thank you." I handed the bottle back.

"Anytime."

An hour later, the vein was ticking on my forehead as Mr. VP threw his weight around *again*.

I crossed my arms in front of me and leaned back. "I'm sorry, I thought you needed my help, that I had some voice in this."

"Ah..." he trailed off, his mouth parted, then abruptly closed. "You do."

"Then you need to let me get a word in edgewise," I ground out. "Otherwise I'm just sitting here like a doll you're throwing words at that mean nothing other than you're saying them."

"What does that mean?" he asked, a little affronted.

"It means right now there is no reason for me to be in this room with you. You're bulldozing right over me." Spelling it out was the only way I was going to get through to him, and with the way his eyes widened, I knew I had.

He sat back in his chair. "I'm sorry. You're right." He held his hand out for me to speak.

"First off, you're talking about one billion dollars in purchases."

His brow scrunched up. "And?"

I couldn't figure out if he was used to talking about such large numbers, or if he really wasn't thinking about the current state of the company. Things were going well, Annex was the third largest content streaming service, but one wrong move and it could all be over.

"One billion is high risk. We have enough to cover some ventures and can get loans for the rest, but that is all leaning on past performance to remain steady. One of the main reasons this company has remained in such good financial standing is because we haven't overstretched available means."

"And that has also kept us behind other giants. We haven't taken large-enough risks," he said.

"Is that your pitch? What are you going to tell them?" I asked. He was thinking like a financial advisor, but not a VP trying to propel the company. Not that it was a bad thing, but there had to be a balance, and I knew he was well aware of that.

Was he testing me?

"What do you think I should tell them?" he asked, his attention solely focused on me.

What would I tell them? The company had its hands in so many buckets that it didn't need to add any more.

"Growth has been steady over the past five years. With the addition of in-house productions, we've doubled. We should invest in producing the hundreds of story rights we own to bring in new membership to help carry the load of the more risky investments. It does us no good to invest in something that shows limited future payback."

It was all about ROI—return on investment. And not everything was that beneficial.

"Wow," he said as he stared at me.

"Wow, what?"

"I'm impressed."

I quirked a brow at him. "Impressed with what?"

He leaned forward and put his elbows on the table. "That you pulled that information from your brain and analyzed the company's cash flow without even a hiccup."

"And?" I asked. I wasn't sure what he was saying.

"It's impressive."

I narrowed my gaze on him. "If you say for a girl, so help me."

He held his hands up. "How about a 'you're right'?"

"Are you about to say you're sorry?" I asked.

He shook his head. "No."

I regarded him for a moment, giving him my best side eye. "Okay, I'll settle for being right."

"I thought it was very big of me," he said as he stood, walking around the corner to my seat.

I turned toward him, my arms still crossed. "There's room for improvement."

He leaned over, placing his hands on the armrests. "Do I get to grope you now?"

My gaze bounced between his eyes, noticing how their blue was dark like the deep parts of the ocean. "It's because we bickered, isn't it?"

He slammed his lips to mine. "Fuck, yes."

Chapter NINE

Natasha

March

After two weeks, Monday through Thursday became simple stepping stones counting down like a clock until I got to see Richard again. I made them productive, if only to keep myself busy, to keep myself from missing him.

It was hard to believe how much I missed him after only being together for a few weeks. Jenna spent a lot of time with Brent, and they sometimes invited me along, but I hated feeling like a third wheel. Also, the baby was zapping my energy and I usually went home and didn't move from my couch.

Of course Richard and I talked on the phone, and texted, and even emailed, but all that did was make me long for him more. I felt the need to be physically connected, surrounded by his arms and breathing him in. I craved him. My skin crawled in desperation for him.

The first week I started sending him memes during the day, but he didn't really understand them, much like the emojis, and it took him a moment to pick up. I had a feeling his office may have been a little too stuffy, and memes weren't a part of his everyday life like they were with mine. Jenna sent me a dozen a day.

Baby Yoda memes were his favorite, and mine as well.

His office, his life, had been too stuffy, and I was happy to be breathing life into him.

Which was why I left early on Friday.

For weeks he'd come down to see me, but it was only fair that I go see him as well. His more flexible schedule had allowed him to leave early, giving us more hours together, but I still had yet to see the condo I might have spent New Year's Day in.

The traffic was insane, and I was happy I clocked out at noon though I didn't tell him I'd left early. The week before he'd given me the pass for his garage and instructions on where to park, and I pulled into a spot right next to his car.

Bag in hand, another passkey for the elevator, and a short walk down the hall to the left, and I was there. Immediately I rang the bell, and my heart thumped with each second before the door swung open.

My heart skipped at the bright blue eyes and blinding smile that met me. He had been working from home all day, and I tried not to linger on the grey sweatpants that were sitting low on his hips, or the white T-shirt covering his chest. It was probably a good thing because I might not have been able to stop myself from dropping to my knees right there if he'd come to the door shirtless.

"Hi," I said.

"Hi." He stepped forward and leaned down, pressing his lips to mine as he took my bag from my hand. "Welcome." He stepped to the side to let me in, and immediately the wall of glass windows exposed nothing but blue. No buildings, no obstructions, just lake.

"So, I was right?" I asked as I stepped through the front door of Richard's sky-high condo, my eyes glued to the view. It really did overlook the lake.

He chuckled and closed the door behind me. "I told you so. Right down to the meal delivery service."

I threw my arms around his neck and he dropped my bag as his arms swept around me, pulling me flush to him.

"Hi," I said with a smile as I stared into his bright blue eyes.

He grinned back at me. "You're early."

I gave a small shrug. "You said the sunsets were spectacular from up here, and that you'd be spending the afternoon working from home."

"I'm just surprised you were able to take off early."

Another shrug. "On one hand is this boss I'm working hard on a project with who wants me to work all the time, and on the other hand is my baby daddy who wants me to take it easy."

"I hate that term."

I smirked at him. I wasn't fond of the name either. "I thought you might. What would you prefer?"

"There are a lot of things I'd prefer, but number one is your boyfriend."

I narrowed my eyes on him. "Hmm, boyfriend, huh?"

"I thought that was established."

I had to admit, I liked to see him sweat a little bit. Honestly, I'd considered him mine since that first weekend. Probably since he wrote it in that text to mystery texter.

"I like the sound of that. So, are you gonna give your girl a tour?"

A groan rumbled in his throat, and he ran his lips up the column of my neck. "I'm sorry, did you say something? I was highly distracted."

I pulled back and rolled my eyes. "Says the man in the grey sweatpants."

"What about my sweatpants?"

"Lift up your shirt."

He followed my instructions and exposed his muscular abdomen and the oh-so-enticing V that disappeared beneath the waistband.

"Damn." I blew out a breath and fanned my face. "Those are totally hot."

"Wait, my sweatpants are hot?"

"Oh, hell, yes. You didn't know that grey sweatpants are the male equivalent of lingerie?"

"You're kidding me."

I shook my head as my eyes moved down. He still hadn't released the hem of his shirt, and I couldn't help but lick my lips at the outline of his cock when it twitched.

"Total aphrodisiac."

He quirked his brow and pushed down on the waistband, a wicked gleam in his eyes as he stared me down.

I blew out a breath and turned. "Plenty of time for that later. Right now, I want to see that view you've teased me about for weeks."

"Tease," he said with a groan, his shirt thankfully covering his skin again. He took my hand and pulled me down the hall, showcasing a half bath, laundry closet, and a bedroom that held his home office and much of his sports memorabilia, with an attached full bathroom.

As soon as we entered the main living area, my mouth dropped open. I saw nothing, none of the room, just the wide expanse of Lake Michigan. I made my way around the furniture until I found the door that led to a balcony. It was cold out, the wind brisk, but I could barely feel it.

"Wow. That's a million-dollar view." It was breathtaking, and the view from the doorway was a pale comparison to the deck.

There was a chuckle behind me, then warm arms encircled me, pulling me close.

"Right on the money."

"That wouldn't surprise me." The noise of Lake Shore Drive floated up over eighteen stories.

"Having this view makes living in the city bearable. I feel less like I'm in a concrete jungle."

"I always thought you loved the city."

He hummed in agreement. "I do, but it's so crammed with people. Sometimes I just want space. All I have to do is put on some headphones, playlist on random, drink in hand, and stare out. Just watch the boats come and go, the sun sparkle on the water."

"So calming," I said. It was much like when I described my favorite color.

He nodded against me and placed a kiss on my shoulder.

I looked to the left down the shoreline, noticing how it curved in the distance. To the right a very familiar sight stuck out into the water, complete with a Ferris wheel. A small giggle left me. I didn't think he heard it.

"Are you going to tell me?" he asked.

"The pier. Where it all started. Where we made a baby."

He hummed against my skin. "Possibly the best night of my life."

"You know I was staying pretty much next door to where you live?"

"Don't tell me that," he said with a groan.

I turned in his arms. "The W."

A growl of frustration left him and his forehead fell against mine. "You've got to be fucking kidding me."

"Yeah."

"Yeah," he said with a shake of his head. He turned me slightly. "You can't see from this angle, but on the other side of the second tower of this complex is the W. It literally is right next door."

I leaned into him, my head resting on his chest. "If only…"

"I should have gone with you."

I shrugged. "Yes, it was lost time, but it was weeks, and now we're together."

"But it was weeks of misunderstanding and not knowing if we would ever see each other again."

I smacked his stomach. "No getting moody on me. I'm here, in your home. Finish this tour, and let's break in that kitchen table."

His hands swept around my back, cupping my ass, giving it a squeeze. "The table, huh?"

"Well somebody's grey sweatpants got me all worked up." I gave him a wink.

A chuckle left him and we moved back inside. There was a nice large living room that was open to a dining room with a fireplace. Around the corner sat the kitchen.

"This kitchen is beautiful." While normally I wasn't fond of galley kitchens, his was nice and wide, and beautifully appointed. A gas burner and double oven, granite counters, and lots of cabinets. "This kitchen is so wasted on you."

At the end sat a large window that almost went from the floor to the ceiling. The dimming of outside light allowed the shine of indoor lighting to be seen, and suddenly the second tower of the property was a full-on peep show.

"Okay, I've lived in apartments for years, but I don't know about this."

"About what?"

I waved at the large pane of glass and the lack of any type of shade. "There are windows, other people, so close that there is no privacy unless your curtains are closed. And I'm not seeing a curtain on this window." I turned to him. "Do you give your neighbors a peep show?"

He stepped forward and hooked his hands around my waist, lifting me until I was sitting on the counter. I drew in a breath as his fingers swept across my panties.

"We could give them a peep show right now."

I bit down on my lip as I wrapped my legs around his waist, pulling him closer. "Mr. Bennett, oh my."

He chuckled before leaning forward and crashing his lips to mine. My whole body lit up as I clawed at him. I reached under his shirt and pressed my hands to his abs and then slipped my hand under his waistband.

He was hot, hard, and silky in my hand. A shuffle of clothing and he swatted my hand away before lining up and slamming in. My head dropped back as every nerve exploded, the blood pumping through my veins flashing away by fire.

"Richard," I mewled as I pulled him closer.

He wasted no time, our eyes locked as he drilled into me. It was fast and dirty and everything I needed right then. Each thrust whited out my mind and amped up the pleasure that rolled through me, ratcheting higher each time he bottomed out until I was hanging onto him for dear life, lost in a sea of ecstasy.

I clung to him, unable to do anything but take him. Every muscle tightened and a low groan left him.

"You wanted to give them a peep show," he growled into my ear. "Fucking show them what I do to you."

His words made the tightness snap and I cried out. He cursed in my ear, his thrusts faltering before he slammed into me one last time. As I came down and the world came back into focus, I pressed light kisses to his neck.

"By the way, Miss Exhibitionist," he said after a minute or two of rest. "The windows are mirrored. You can't see in."

My mouth popped open and I glanced over to all the lights I'd seen in the building next to us. That was when I noticed that what I had seen was the light shining from an open window and the sun reflecting.

Whoops.

"Well, just the thought of it was hot," I said. Which was incredibly true. Maybe I was a bit of an exhibitionist. If I was, I totally blamed it on him.

"As hot as my sweatpants?" he asked as he brushed my hair back.

I bit down on my lips as I glanced down to where we were still joined. "Mmm, those are definitely hotter."

"Then, speaking of lingerie…" he trailed off, his eyes glancing to a box sitting on the end of the counter. "I know it won't fit for long, but I got you a little surprise that I would *love* for you to model for me later."

"Did you, now? Hmm, I supposed I could do that, but you've got to keep these pants on."

He pressed his lips to mine. "Deal."

The next morning I let out a contented sigh, my head on Richard's chest, listening to the steady swoosh of his heart. It was one of those bliss-filled mornings you wished you could bottle. The sun was shining, I was certain birds were chirping somewhere but we were too high up, and I was a boneless body draped over the man that I had *very* strong feelings for.

With each breath there was a hint of spice from his cologne, and I snuggled in a little closer to his warmth. The light touch of his fingertips tracing shapes up and down my arm only furthered my descent into blissville.

"We should probably get up," I whispered, to which he gave a small hum that vibrated in his chest. "There is supposed to be sightseeing and dates and having fun." Another hum. I wanted to give him a playful smack, but couldn't seem to muster the energy to even lift my fingers. "We can't just have sex all weekend."

"Why not?"

A small zing of pleasure moved through me. His morning voice was pure sexual stimulation—deep, full of gravel, with that edge of constant command it always held.

Unfortunately, his question felt very valid. The baby was zapping my energy a lot lately, and as much as I wanted to do the touristy things, I also just wanted to stay all nice and cozy wrapped up in him.

Somehow I managed to muster enough energy to tilt my head back. "Your son is hungry."

"My son? You mean my daughter."

I loved our little disagreement on the gender of our baby. "I thought you'd be hoping for a boy."

"Of course I'd like a boy. I'd also like a girl."

I shook my head. "I'm not having twins."

"In that case we'll have one this time, then next time try for the other," he said, and my heart skipped.

"Next time, huh?"

"I guess that may be a little early." There was such conviction in his voice I knew I wasn't the only one falling hard in this relationship. Early, yes, but my heart leapt at the knowledge that he was already seeing us together years down the road.

"Maybe, but I have to tell you something."

"What's that?" he asked.

I smiled up at him. "How happy I am with you."

He craned his neck to look down at me, his hand moving to cup my face, a small smile playing on his lips and a softness in his gaze. "Me too."

All of our grand plans of seeing the city gave way to being snuggled under blankets on the sofa while binge watching movies on Annex and ordering takeout. His phone rang a few times, causing us to have to pause whatever we were watching, but I didn't mind.

I couldn't remember the last time I enjoyed just *being* with a boyfriend. We hadn't been together long, but as I stared into his eyes while we talked late into the morning it hit me—love.

I was already in love with him.

Chapter TEN

Richard

Mid March

I stared down at my phone, at the photo I'd taken at Natasha's the weekend before. Natasha was asleep, her arm thrown up above her head, breasts covered by the sheet.

How many years had it been since I had felt this way about a woman? Since I could barely stand being away from a girlfriend or my wife for more than a few hours?

Searching my memory, I could find none. Perhaps some from high school came close, but the woman had my mind wandering in the middle of the day. She had me working long into the night so that I could leave early just to see her sooner. I didn't tell her that, though. I couldn't.

Only a month had passed, but it felt like multiple months. There was never the usual period of awkwardness. It felt like she knew the deepest parts of me without even trying. And if she didn't, she could force them out of me. It was amazing and freeing, and frightening as hell.

A knock sounded at my door and I cleared the screen, but not without one last longing glance at my beauty.

"Come in."

"Hey, man," Keenan said with a grin as he walked in and sat in one of the chairs in front of my desk.

"Is it lunch already?" I asked.

He nodded. "When you weren't in the lobby, I figured I needed to come pry you away from those spreadsheets you love so much. Though I gotta say, I don't think it's those that have got you grinning like a fool."

My eyes flashed open and I quickly fixed my expression, pulling my mouth into a neutral line.

He shook his head. "Not gonna help, man. I saw that lovey-dovey look in your eye. That girl has you wrapped around her little finger." He twirled his finger in the air.

"That's not it," I argued, though he was correct.

"Nothing to be defensive about. Love looks good on you."

Love. Fuck.

Natasha and I hadn't been together long. "Too soon for that."

Keenan's brow scrunched. "No, it's not. You've been in love with her since that night. Your incessant whining when she didn't contact you back was enough to tell me that."

I narrow my gaze on him. "I was not incessantly whining."

"Maybe. Thing is, you've been obsessed with her since that night. You talked about her nonstop for a week, and you never do that shit. Not even with Desiree, and you married her."

"Worst decision of my life," I grumbled.

"Hey, at least you got out of it before you got high up the corporate ladder. Unlike me, having to split my contract."

"And now you're a working stiff like me." It was a joke we volleyed around, but the truth was Keenan was pretty much set for retirement. I'd made sure of it. Investments that created a steady income. I got him in on Annex when they were up and coming, before I worked for them, and even had him invest in a few fast food franchises.

"Nah, I ain't like you. Honestly, you lost the dream."

"That dream was shattered with my body, remember?"

"That's a hit I'll never forget. What I'm saying is you sit here all day working your ass off, making the money, but you have no life, no joy in your heart. This chick gives you that joy in a way I've never seen in you. It may be early, but that doesn't mean it ain't real."

"I think I'm still in a bit of shock that it's all real. I'm going to be a dad."

He nodded. "I may talk shit about my ex, but she's a good mom and we made some fantastic kids. You're going to be a great dad. How's that going to work, by the way? Is she going to move up here?"

I stood and pulled my jacket from the hanger. "We haven't really gotten to talk about all that yet, but I assume she'll move up here. I can switch her to another department in the company."

He nodded. "Not a bad plan, but I'd talk it out with her soon."

"We're still getting to know each other. There's still time."

We headed out of my office and down the hall toward the elevator. I gave Michael, the CEO, a wave as I passed his office, and he held up his sandwich. I couldn't help but shake my head. The man rarely left his office for lunch.

"By the way, I've got box seats to the Cubs opening day if you want to take KJ and Mina," I said as we walked down the block toward our usual deli spot.

"Really? That would be awesome. Thanks."

"No problem." We stepped into the crowded restaurant, and immediately I stopped.

Heading out the door walking straight for me was a figure I hadn't seen in six years. Despite living in the same city as my ex-wife, I'd managed never to run into her until then.

"Rick."

I looked up and locked gazes with a familiar set of green eyes. Eyes that I'd spent hours looking into. Eyes that I'd believed when she told me she loved me.

She wasn't alone. There was a stroller in front of her with a bouncing toddler and my ex-best friend standing beside her with a small girl in his arms.

"Desiree. Andy," I said.

My fists clenched at my side. Even after seven years, the sight of them made my blood boil. Their betrayal hit harder than anything else in my life.

"How are you doing?" Desiree asked, tension building between us.

I nodded, my jaw clenched. "I'm good. You two look well." The air was stilted, awkward, and I knew I was the cause.

They glanced at each other, a look I remember seeing so many times and brushed it off as nothing. The obviousness of it was like a knife in the chest, reminding me what love could do, how it could shred your insides.

"What are you up to these days?" Andy asked.

"Work, mostly."

"Are you married? Kids?" Desiree's hopeful edge rubbed me wrong.

Natasha flashed in my mind, the barely there bump of our baby. "No."

"But he's got one on the way," Keenan said from beside me.

I shot Keenan a death glare before looking at the fucking genuinely happy smile on Desiree's face.

"That's so wonderful!"

"She's still in the first trimester, so we're not really telling anyone yet." I gave Keenan the side eye and clenched my jaw at his nonchalant attitude.

"The fall will be here before you know it," Desiree said, already having worked out the rough due date. "I'm happy for you, Rick. I really wish you nothing but happiness."

"Thanks." It was all I could muster as I caught a glimpse of her wedding band. So different from the one I'd given her.

She gave me an awkward smile. "We should be going. It was so good seeing you again, Rick."

I clenched my jaw and gave a curt nod before watching them walk past in their happy little family bubble.

Keenan and I were seated at a high-back booth, and I ordered a bourbon before the hostess even left. I didn't give a single fuck that it wasn't her job, someone was getting me a fucking drink.

"They looked good," Keenan said, completely ignoring the anger I knew was all over my face.

"Right out of a fucking magazine. Doesn't fucking matter what they had to do to get there, who and what they destroyed."

"Cool it down, man."

I glared up at him. "I can't be pissed because she's happy?"

"It's been seven years," he reminded me.

It didn't help. All seven years had done was allow the anger to stew, and seeing them together just stirred it all up again. Dusted off the memories, the pain and anger. "I fucking know. But to see them like that. Married. Kids. To see them happy and lovey knowing what they did to get there. How they fucked me over. Lied to me over and over. Why was I the victim in it all and I'm still getting punched?"

"I get it, man, but you can't keep this negativity on you. All it's going to do is fuck you up. You've got a kick-ass girl and a baby on the way. Screw them. Let go of all that shit and remember what you have."

"What do I have? A woman I barely know that I fucking knocked up because I was thinking with my dick."

Keenan's hand slammed down on the table. "Don't fucking do that. Don't put her down because you're still pissed off at your ex. I know that's not how you feel."

He was right. I was letting my anger run right over my feelings for Natasha. I didn't mean the words, not at all, but my mouth still spouted the shit.

Natasha was a breath of life. Inquisitive and quirky and sweet and witty, and so very different from Desiree in all the right ways. All the perfect ways, and she was carrying my baby. *My* baby.

"I didn't mean…" I blew out a breath, but it did little to settle the turmoil that heaved inside my chest.

It *was* my baby, right?

"I know you didn't, but you need a fucking smack upside the head for saying that shit. She's not Desiree, so don't try and put her in that same box."

I nodded in agreement, but even then doubt began to weave. My chest tightened and my leg bounced.

My phone went off, and I answered it without even looking at the number.

"Hello," I said in a brisk tone. There was a pause, and I was so close to hitting the end button when a soft voice came over the line.

"Hello. I'm looking for my boyfriend, Richard. Have you seen him?" Natasha said.

I blew out a breath, and I felt my body relax back in the seat. "I'm sorry." And I meant that for more than just the attitude I answered the phone with. I also meant it for the venomous words I said about her in anger at my ex-wife.

"You wanna tell me what has you all in a huff?"

"Not particularly."

She blew out a breath. "Okay, let's try this again. What's wrong? What happened? And don't brush me off."

It was so infuriating when she did that, when she forced me to tell her things I didn't want to talk about, but I did it. Always. Because she asked, and she was also perceptive and hard to keep anything from. Tenacious in her quest to know me.

It was scary to open myself up, but I couldn't stop myself from telling her anything.

Even the hardest things.

Even in the middle of a restaurant at lunch. The walls of the booth were high, at least six feet, and I pushed myself into the corner, my voice low as I spoke.

"It's…I…I ran into Desiree and Andy."

"And they are?" she asked.

I blinked, realizing my error—I'd never mentioned their names. "My ex-wife and my ex-best friend."

"Oh."

I'd told her some of what happened, but a glossy explanation of how my marriage exploded didn't do the emotions justice.

"Yeah, so, not a great lunch."

"They were together." It was a statement, like she was putting together the pieces I was grindingly handing out.

"Yes."

"After all these years."

"With two kids," I elaborated.

"That had to hurt," she said softly, making my chest ache.

"Yes and no. The hurt came from the memories of the pain, of having given myself to someone so completely only to be betrayed by the two people closest to me. Then, to see they're living happily ever after and I'm still lost in the aftermath."

Somehow the spilling out released the tension, and it felt like the pressure building inside me was leaking out from an unseen valve.

Keenan pointed to the menu as the waiter had arrived and I nodded as he pointed to a sandwich I often ordered.

"Thank you."

"For what?" I asked. She should not have been thanking me, not with the way I was acting.

"Telling me. I know it's hard for you."

And I felt even shittier that I let myself even say, let alone think, those things about her, even for a fraction of a second.

Natasha wasn't Desiree, and she'd given me absolutely no reason to distrust her.

"I caught them in bed together. In our bed," I said, opening up more. With each word, more of that pressure subsided.

"That had to be awful seeing that."

"They were done with *that*. There were voices coming from

our bedroom, and when I got there I heard them talking about a future together, one that excluded me. At which point I stepped in and said that it could be arranged," I said, my jaw clenching. "What hurt more was there was no fanfare. It was easy for her to walk away, to start over, but it wasn't easy for me. I buried myself in work and tried to forget, but the hurt never went away."

It was cathartic to tell her, to let her know some of the darkest parts of me.

"Why does it still bother you so much?" she asked. "I can tell you're upset, I can hear it in your voice."

Why did it? Even I wasn't sure. "I don't know how to answer that."

"Are you still in love with her?" There was a shake in her voice, and I didn't like that.

"No," I said forcefully. I'd long ago let that feeling die out.

"Then what is it? Why does seeing her affect you so?" As she pressed on I realized she needed to know as much as I needed to tell her, though I didn't want to.

"Because they were the two people I loved most in the world, people I thought loved me, but they didn't," I ground out.

There was silence for a moment. "That pain will always be there when you think back on it, but you can't let it rule you. Don't give it power."

Could she be any more perfect? "Thanks. What can I do for you, Dr. Cates?"

She chuckled, and if she had been in front of me, I knew she'd be rolling her eyes. "I just wanted to let you know that I miss you."

"You called just to tell me that?" I asked, my chest warming.

"And I wanted to hear your voice," she said softly.

I ran my hand through my hair. "I miss you, too. More than you know." *More than I can even comprehend.*

Meeting Natasha was like being hit by the L—life changing. Little by little I was becoming someone new with her.

Now the trouble was not fucking things up.

Chapter ELEVEN

Natasha

For weeks I'd heard the whispered words and theories, Jenna had even filled me in on some of the gossip circulating on her side of the building. I tried not to let it get to me, but every time Richard popped up, he didn't care who saw us being affectionate. It negated all of my efforts to appear professional.

However, I felt a change occurring in my relationship with Richard. Work Richard, the VP, was serious and stiff, while my boyfriend was loving and attentive. The problem was the VP was becoming more and more present with each week.

Earlier in the week I sent him our favorite baby Yoda memes, and twice in the week he hadn't responded. One night I even went without our nightly phone call. It wasn't like our nightly calls were long and time consuming, sometimes they were as short as a couple of minutes, but it was enough just to hear his voice.

It felt like our footing had become uneven somehow, but I attributed it to the distance between us.

"Natasha, did I hear Richard was coming down today?" Marjorie asked as she appeared in my cubicle.

Marjorie used to only be someone I ran into in the break room or bathroom or the occasional meeting, but she started popping up more and more. It was getting on my nerves and I was beginning to understand Richard's frustration with her. She seemed to be focused on finding me or my department doing something wrong so she could turn me in.

Like an overly nosy neighbor, she was constantly watching.

I clenched my teeth before turning in my chair and looking up at her. "He is."

"Did you know it's against company policy to have relations with a subordinate?" she asked.

My expression fell, and my jaw ticked, finally understanding her interest. "Yes, I am aware of that."

"And do you know the penalty?"

Was she threatening me? I stood and was sadly unable to be eye-to-eye with her. "Excuse me?"

"Natasha!" Richard's voice called out and I turned to find him walking toward us, his steely gaze on Marjorie.

"Hello, Richard," Marjorie said, a slight waver in her voice.

"Marjorie. What brings you to Natasha?" he asked. I could tell by the hard set of his jaw he was ready to lash out at her.

"Just a friendly chat."

I made a humph sound, and Richard's gaze flickered to me.

"There is no time for friendly chats today. Natasha is already late for our meeting."

I picked up my laptop and the files I needed, and stepped around Marjorie. She didn't have any response, probably too embarrassed she was almost caught trying to intimidate me.

"Thank you," I said as the door closed.

"Are you going to tell me what that was all about?"

I sat down and opened up my laptop. "Just Marjorie being Marjorie." If she thought she could threaten me, she had another thing coming. Richard was the Vice President, and I wasn't going to lose my job because we were dating, despite what she might think.

"That's all?"

I nodded. "So, I gathered up the last year's profit and loss statements, and I think I found a way to make the more sound investments work with the budget without overstretching the company too much."

He stared at me for a moment, then took the seat next to me. "Tell me more."

We spent the next few hours solidifying the plan. There were only a few short weeks left until his meeting when everything we'd gathered would be presented.

We ended up leaving the office after everyone else had gone. It was eerie to be there alone with him.

His arms wrapped around my waist and he nuzzled my neck. "The things I could do to you right now."

A giggle left me, then my stomach let out a roar, making us both laugh.

"Guess I should get my girls some food first."

We headed back to my place, and before he could start looking at restaurants I began pulling ingredients from the fridge. I was determined to cook.

Things had changed in me due to the pregnancy, and I found myself getting lightheaded if I didn't eat every few hours—even if it was just a handful of crackers.

It was a hard-learned lesson when Jenna and I were at the grocery store. My heart started to race, and my hands were shaking, then the room started to spin.

Thank goodness for Jenna catching me before I fell. I needed to remember to mention it to my doctor the next time I saw her.

"Are you okay?" Richard asked as he stared at me.

I'd been so focused on my task and our meeting that I'd forgotten to eat my snack. My hands vibrated and my heart was flying in my chest. I wiped my hands off on the towel and moved to sit at the kitchen table, Richard in step behind me.

"Natasha, what's wrong?" He crouched down in front of me, his brow furrowed as he placed his hands on my knees.

I closed my eyes and gripped onto his shoulders, praying I didn't pass out.

"Baby, you're scaring me."

Blindly, I reached for the sleeve of saltines sitting on the table and immediately popped one in my mouth. Richard seemed to understand and pulled a Sprite from the fridge, popping the top before handing it to me. I took a few greedy sips, then devoured another cracker, and another. By the fifth cracker and half a can of soda, the shaking had subsided considerably.

"I'm okay. I just forgot to eat a snack," I assured him. And I was fine…for the most part. "It's just more of the lovely side effects of growing a human."

He brushed back a lock of hair from my face. "Are you sure?"

I nodded. "Positive."

"Have you told your doctor about this?" He covered my hands with his, giving them a squeeze.

I shook my head. "I see her on Tuesday. They didn't have a Friday appointment." I crunched down on another cracker.

If the symptoms continued throughout the rest of my pregnancy, I was really going to need to make sure I carried snacks with me at all times.

"I'm ordering dinner," he said as he pulled out his phone and scanned the options.

"No, I can finish. We can't keep going out for every meal," I argued as I got up to continue chopping vegetables. I'd been looking up recipes all week and was excited to try a Mexican shredded beef one I'd found.

"It's not worth you falling over. And why not?" Richard was the king of takeout and food delivery services, but that wasn't something I was used to. However, I did find him to be a master onion dicer. That was when he revealed his mom was a cook at a local restaurant in the town he grew up in who taught him many things around the kitchen.

"Because I'm growing every day, and that is just more calories than I need. Besides, I like to cook."

"I don't mind cooking," he said, which I found surprising.

"But you never do it. Interesting."

He shrugged. "My father didn't like me being in the kitchen with my mom and sister and often dragged me outside to help chop wood or some other more 'manly' task."

"Okay. Why did he do that?" It was another piece to the Richard puzzle.

"Because I was a boy. He expected his son to be a man and let women do softer tasks. My father isn't the most open with his emotions."

"That's where you get it from."

He shook his head and pulled me closer, his lips pressing against my forehead. "Compared to him, I am an open book."

"Tell me about your sister," I said. I'd been hoping he would open up about his family, but it was like pulling teeth to get any information out of him. "You don't talk much about your family, but I feel like she's the safest topic."

"Susie is a lesbian living her dreams with her partner in California far from the scrutiny of our parents," he said.

"Okay, that was the most basic explanation I've ever heard."

He shrugged. "She's a pediatrician who fell in love with one of her nurses."

"Oh, how scandalous."

"It really was. Suz came out to me when she was fifteen. She knew even then, but she didn't tell our parents until she was in college."

"Were you two close back then?" I asked.

He nodded. "We were, but when I went off to college, I'll admit I wasn't the best at keeping in touch. Then she went off to college and med school, and next thing I know she's living on the other side of the country."

I took another sip, finishing off the Sprite. "Do you talk?"

"Thanks to the advent of video chats, we've actually gotten closer the last…well, since I got divorced." He picked up the book

I'd been reading, one of those what-to-expect pregnancy books. After the initial shock wore off, I craved knowledge about what was happening in my body. Especially knowledge about when some of my symptoms might stop.

He flipped through the pages, stopping at one I'd bookmarked with a sticky note.

"Your baby is the size of a strawberry," he read out. His eyes met mine, and I bit down on my lower lip. "We're going to have a girl."

"Oh we are, are we?" It had become a running gag, but I secretly hoped he was right.

He nodded, confident in his statement. "A little princess who will adore her daddy."

"Well, just to be a pain, I'm going to say we're having a boy."

"A boy after we have a little girl."

I rolled my eyes at him. "How many kids do you think we're going to have?"

He grinned at me. "At least—"

His phone went off, which was something that had been happening more and more lately. He grimaced and excused himself to answer. With him distracted, I was able to continue cooking and avoid another take-out meal.

Chapter TWELVE

Richard

End of March

I SHOULD HAVE STAYED AT THE OFFICE.

I should have been in a meeting with Michael about next month's rollout.

But instead I was where I wanted to be, though the quirked brow and pursed lips that met me had me on edge. Natasha was still working, and I wasn't even there for the project we were working on together.

"In the five years I've worked here I don't think you've ever come for a visit, but the last month and a half you've come five times," she said before standing. "I think I'm getting special attention, because Nina never saw you this much. And if you're blaming it on my department I will swat you."

I had been to the office before, many times, but it was odd how I'd never seen or noticed her. If she hadn't been in that meeting, would I have noticed that day?

"No, I'm blaming it on you."

She rolled her eyes, a smile playing on her lips. "Ass." I pulled on her wrist and she crashed against my chest. "Richard," she hissed, her gaze darting around.

I didn't give a fuck who saw or who knew. She was mine. "By Wednesday my skin crawls, aching for your touch. When Friday rolls around I can't stand being away from you anymore."

I wanted to be around her all the time. The distance was really starting to grate on me.

"There are still two hours until the weekend starts," she said, thinking that would deter me, but it wasn't going to work.

"And you've already worked forty," I pointed out, making sure she knew I was watching.

"How do you know that?"

I grinned at her. "Baby, I'm the VP—I know all. Besides, I actually came to pick you up."

"Pick me up?"

My lips formed a thin line. "I just got out of a meeting with Derek in acquisitions, and then I wanted to take you back to Chicago."

"Chicago?"

I nodded. "I have a conference call tomorrow I can't miss, and some work to do."

I hated the flicker of disappointment in her eyes just before she looked away. "Why didn't you just stay there and work, then come when you were done?"

Because I'm addicted to you.

"I wanted to see you, and if I went back there I might not have been able to tear myself away from my computer because you aren't there to do your little siren song and pull me away."

"My siren song, huh?"

I nodded. "Very siren-y."

"Does it bring all the boys to the yard?" she asked, that sexy smirk I loved so much on her lips.

"It brings my boys."

"Hey, hottie McHotterson, what are you doing here?" Jenna asked, emerging from the open door to the break room.

"Picking up Natasha. What are you doing here?"

She rolled her eyes at me. "I might be working, but sometimes I really don't know."

"Might want to figure that out before your boss notices," I said with a chuckle.

"The only thing she notices is if I'm violating some arbitrary office policy that nobody cares about and everyone breaks, including her boss."

While I appreciated rules and order, they were never as black and white as Marjorie took them to be. The morale of her section was low and was something I needed to investigate. The last thing we wanted to do was lose good employees due to bad management.

I knew Natasha didn't exactly like the office knowing about us, and I began to wonder how much Marjorie had to do with that.

Wrangling Natasha from the office was almost as bad as pulling me from mine, but with Jenna's assistance I got her to her car and I saw a look pass between them. Jenna's eyes went wide and then glanced toward me, but Natasha gave a small shake of her head. It was odd.

"What?" I asked.

Jenna and I stared at Natasha, who glared at her best friend. "It's nothing," she said before sliding into the driver's side.

I exchanged a look with Jenna, one that gave nothing away, before climbing into my own car. The interaction didn't sit well with me and different scenarios played out in my head on the drive to her apartment.

The last person to keep secrets from me was fucking my best friend, sneaking around behind my back for years. What was Natasha keeping from me?

Once at her apartment, I watched her pull an overnight bag from her closet, the same one she'd brought when she visited, and she began stuffing it with clothes and any of the necessary items she might need.

I managed to keep my hands from her, but when I noticed the slope of her abdomen, the definite bump, there was nothing that could keep me from her. Stepping up behind her, I wrapped my arms around her, one hand resting on her bump.

She was so tiny in my arms. When she wasn't wearing heels she was almost a foot shorter than me, and I had to admit I loved how my arms swallowed her up.

"Hi," she said with a small laugh at my sudden attack.

I just grunted back as I held her in my arms, my thumb stroking her bump as I placed a kiss to her neck. The change in her body in just a few weeks was amazing. In six weeks she went from flat to a cute little curve that was evidence of our baby.

"How are you feeling?" I asked, my lips pressing against her temple.

"Not bad. Now that I'm in my second trimester I can hopefully start kissing this exhaustion goodbye."

A few minutes later we were loaded up in my car and on the road. It sucked to do a there and back in one day, but to spend more time with her, I would do it.

We weren't very far out of Indianapolis when Natasha went silent. When I glanced over, her eyes were closed and her lips were parted. It seemed she was going to have to wait a little bit longer for the exhaustion to abate.

With another glance, I noticed the dark circles around her eyes. She looked somehow smaller as well, her skin paler. How had I not noticed earlier?

I knew the pregnancy had drained her energy, reduced her to taking naps the moment she got home, and she'd had some trouble keeping food down. But by the look of her, there was more. That, or I simply hadn't noticed the toll the pregnancy was taking on her. It wasn't something I had to think much about, and I didn't see her daily to know.

My chest clenched, and I realized how much I wanted to take care of this woman…this woman who was giving me a gift that I never thought I'd experience.

I didn't know what the answer was to our problem, but we would find it.

There was always some position opening up in the Chicago office. The idea of her as my personal assistant crossed my mind, but that was more fantasy based than reality based.

If she moved up to Chicago, she wouldn't even need to work after the baby was born. We could get a three-bedroom condo, or even a four bedroom for future children. That way, I still retained a home office.

I hoped she'd like that, like Chicago, because I hated when we were apart, even after only six weeks.

There was a calm that came over me when she was near. A peace I hadn't felt in ages. Maybe Keenan's words weren't far off. Maybe there was so much more to us than I'd comprehended.

From the moment I met her, I'd known she was different. She was more of everything, and I wanted all of her.

All of the sudden it was difficult to breathe. I found myself almost having to pull over from the pain constricting my chest.

It was a pain I'd known for many years, rearing its ugly head, reminding me what those types of thoughts could do. Those feelings that had once crushed me were growing again, for her.

And that scared me.

I couldn't do it. I couldn't give her that kind of power over me. I wouldn't.

I felt it then, the first barrier as it slipped into place, shielding my heart from that pain again.

Chapter
THIRTEEN

Natasha

There was a strange feeling in the air when I woke up shortly before we arrived deep in the heart of downtown Chicago. Almost as if there was an invisible wall that had been erected between us, dividing the car in two. It hadn't been there before, and its appearance now was a foreshadowing that made my heart ache.

"Why don't you go take a nap," Richard said after we walked in.

"I just woke up."

He nodded. "What sounds good for dinner?"

I brushed my hair behind my ear, my brow furrowing. I didn't like the distance in his gaze but what scared me was the physical distance that he placed between us. This wasn't the same man who dropped in to my office hours ago. What had happened when I was asleep?

"Pasta. Does that work?"

He nodded and walked into the kitchen and the drawer where he stored menu copies. "There's an Italian restaurant that's good."

I watched as he flipped through them, his concentration focused until he found what he was looking for. He handed me the menu before his attention turned to his phone.

I glanced at it. Some ricotta stuffed shells sounded good. Along with a side salad and breadsticks, and some tiramisu for dessert.

"Do you know what you want?" I asked.

He nodded and turned his phone toward me, showing off the online menu. "I've already got my order in. What do you want?"

I rattled off my order, knowing I wasn't going to be able to eat half of it, but pasta always made great leftovers.

"Thirty to forty-five minutes," he said before moving to the bedroom.

The air was stifled between us and I didn't understand why. I watched as he changed clothes and admired the way his muscles moved. All the while I yearned for the space between us to disappear.

He barely looked at me as he moved past me. I grabbed his arm and stopped him. "Are you okay?"

"Fine." He pulled me close, but it wasn't the warm swaddling I was used to. It was stiff, and the kiss to my forehead was mechanical. "I'll be in my office."

But things weren't fine. I practically ate alone, and went to bed alone. When I woke in the middle of the night, the balcony door was open and he was sitting, staring out into the darkness of the lake. The full moon bounced off the glassy surface and in the distance, lights twinkled.

"Hi," I said as I stepped outside.

He started, his head snapping in my direction as he drew in a breath. "Hi."

"What are you doing out here?" I moved to stand in front of him, trying not to shiver in the cool air.

His brow furrowed, and he opened up the comforter surrounding him, beckoning me forward. I straddled his hips, my hands resting on his chest, and earned a groan from him before he wrapped the blanket around me.

"You shouldn't be out here. I don't want you getting sick."

I cupped his neck with my hands. "I could say the same thing. How long have you been out here?"

He shook his head. "I'm not sure."

I moved my hands up to his ears and gasped at how cold they were, so I kept my hands in place to help warm them up.

His arms wrapped tighter around me, pulling me closer, and he let out a sigh as he rested his head in the crook of my neck.

"Are you going to tell me what's wrong?"

"I just…got locked in my head. I'm sorry."

"It's okay," I assured him. Though I could tell that wasn't all of it. Something had shaken him, and maybe it was all an internal struggle, but I could tell pressuring him to open up on this one wasn't going to go well.

Whatever the subject, it was something he had to work out at his own pace. While I didn't like that, I did feel a little bit better about his behavior, even if I didn't approve of him brushing me off. I'd give him some slack.

I pulled back to find his eyes in the moonlight. They shone bright blue even in the dim light. His forehead was wrinkled, and I smoothed the lines away. He was so handsome, and every time I looked at him, I was awestruck that he was mine.

"Just don't forget about me."

His brow furrowed again, deeper, almost sad. "I could never forget about you. Not ever for the rest of my life."

My heart skipped and I closed the distance between us, my lips pressing lightly to his. Low in his chest, a hum vibrated. His hands moved down my back to my thighs, running down to my knees and back up to the hem of his T-shirt, which I was wearing.

"I love how tiny you look in my shirt," he whispered against my lips while his fingers kneaded my ass.

He stretched up to capture my mouth, his tongue brushing against mine. Another moan vibrated in his chest and he pulled me down harder onto his lap, the hard edge of his cock rubbing against my clit.

I drew in a sharp breath, my hips rotating against him. Each twist of my hips had me whimpering into his mouth.

I slid my hands between us, slipping them under the waistband of his sweatpants. He jumped when I wrapped my hand around his hard shaft. He nipped at my neck as I pulled him out. I lifted my hips and pushed my panties to the side.

His eyes locked with mine, lips parted as I sank down on him. It took a couple of tries before I was fully seated.

"Fuck," he groaned before raising his hips. He held me tighter to his chest as I slowly rose up, then fell back down to meet his thrusts.

It was slow and sensual, and I felt our connection again.

With one hand he held me in place and began to thrust up harder and faster. His lips ghosted my parted ones as we breathed each other in.

Another groan as he buried his head into my neck again, his hand tangled in my hair, pulling my head back as he licked and kissed, little sharp nips of his teeth as the pace picked up.

"Natasha," he whispered before a strangled sound left him. He slammed his hips up and pulled me down until there was no space between us.

I felt each twitch as he emptied inside me. I rested my head against his shoulder as he came down. Light kisses peppered my cheek and neck.

"I'm sorry," he whispered.

"It's okay, just…talk to me."

He nodded, and when I tried to sit up, he held me to him. "Not yet."

I reached up and caressed his cheek. "Okay."

We sat there for a while, so long that I was jostled awake by Richard standing. He held me close as he carried me inside and placed me on the bed, where I promptly fell right back to sleep.

"Dinner is here," I said. There was no response, so I walked over to Richard's office and leaned on the door frame as I waited for him to look over from his computer screen.

As much as I loved coming to his house, I wasn't too happy about only seeing him for a quickie on the deck at two in the morning. Sadly, that was how it had been since we arrived on Friday.

All day Saturday he was locked away in his office while I lounged on the couch and surfed movies on Annex all by myself. Not much different than what I would be doing at home, but I would have preferred to be wrapped up in him while we watched. Just have him near.

Around noon he came up for air and a quick bite, and a promise of just a few more minutes with a quick kiss before disappearing for hours again.

By five, I was going through the menus and getting his opinion before ordering.

"Mr. Bennett, your food is getting cold," I said after ten minutes of him ignoring my call to come to dinner once it arrived.

"Don't call me that," he said coolly.

My spine straightened at his tone. "Excuse me?" The weekend had me at highs and lows, and I was ready to have it out if need be.

His jaw twitched, and he turned to me. "If you call me that again, you'll set me off and I'll fuck you into the wall and won't stop until you're coming all over my cock again and again, and you won't be able to stand when I'm done."

I breathed a sigh of relief. "Taking your frustrations out on me won't help."

He leaned back into his chair and blew out a breath before running his hands down his face. "I should go down to the gym."

I shook my head and walked over to him. "You should shut that off and come eat. Spend some time with your girlfriend."

He leaned forward, his head resting on my small bump. It was one of those moments that I knew no matter what was going on, he needed me. Even if it was just to run my fingers through his hair. A small comfort, but it seemed enough to calm him.

He stood and placed a quick kiss to my lips before taking my hand and pulling me toward the kitchen.

"Come on. My little girl said she's hungry."

"Oh, I see how it is. I ask and get threatened with hot, frustration-fueled sex, but when your son asks, you're out of your chair in a fraction of a second."

Finally his eyes softened, as did the line of his mouth, and his shoulders relaxed a tiny bit. "It's my job to keep my girls fed."

The air cleared a bit more as we ate. He seemed to relax as we worked hard on a deep dish from Gino's East. I could get them in the freezer section at the grocery store now, but there was nothing that compared to a fresh-made, hot Gino's pizza.

"So, football was your dream, and sadly that crashed and burned early," I said in my quest to know more about the man who'd stolen my heart, despite his recent irritable personality.

"Correct."

I sawed into my piece, practically salivating. Hunger had taken over. It'd been weeks since I'd been this hungry. "And then you went on to get a degree in finance, then an MBA."

"Yes."

"Was being a VP of Finance your goal?" I asked.

He shook his head before spearing a piece of pepperoni from my plate with a smirk. I stared at him with what I was certain was "you did not just steal a pregnant woman's pepperoni" look and got only a cheeky smile in return.

Too bad I couldn't have a beer. Nothing went better with Chicago-style pizza than a cider ale.

"I wasn't really sure what I wanted to do. I was good with numbers, it was something that made money, so it seemed logical."

In retaliation, I stole the remainder of his breadstick. "If you could use your degree for anything, what would you do?"

"I miss football."

"You can't use your degree for football."

That made him chuckle, and he shook his head. "I see these players that came from nothing get offered more money than they could ever dream of, then they get hurt and they've blown all their money. Or they are just bad at money and are making millions a season and are broke."

"Don't they have advisers?" I asked.

He shook his head. "They get some financial planning help, but not enough, in my mind. Keenan played ten years for the NFL. He was a lower-paid player, but he was with the NFL, and what he got was still millions."

"Is that how you two met?"

He shook his head as he chewed his bite. "No, we played together in college. He was on the field when I went down, was the first standing over me, calling help over. But when he got signed, I went to him and we put in a plan for him to have a sustainable future outside the game. He was never going to be one of those names everyone knew, and that was fine by him because he was doing what he loved."

"What did you do to help?" I asked. In the last few months Keenan was the only friend I'd ever heard Richard talk about. And it was a true friendship, not a work one or a casual one.

"Okay, one thing I had him do was invest in Annex."

My eyes popped open wide. "That's insider trading."

He held up his hand. "It would have been, but it was years before Michael came to me. Streaming content was the future, and Keenan agreed. I also had him purchase a fast food franchise. Then when that made money, another one. He owns four stores now that keep him in a steady income that he just plugs into savings."

"What about his divorce?" That had to have hit hard.

"Thank fuck he listened to me and got a prenup, though he still took a few hits financially. But so many of those guys don't know the first thing about any of it. Some have money for the first time in their lives and suddenly blow millions on houses and cars and jewelry, then a year later they're out of the game."

I hadn't ever really heard him talk about anything with such conviction before. It was obvious it was a subject close to his heart. And I loved seeing that side of him. The part always buried by the business-minded VP.

"That sounds like something you're passionate about."

He gave me a shy smile and looked down at his plate. "It is. I feel like it has value. I loved helping Keenan and seeing him financially stable."

"Are there companies out there that do stuff like that?"

He nodded. "There is at least one I know of."

It made me wonder. If he was so passionate about it, what was holding him back from doing it?

"You've been married to your job for so long you haven't even thought about anything outside of it."

"I do get enjoyment from my job, despite the hours and bullshit I have to put up with." He chuckled and aimed his fork at another piece of pepperoni, but I managed to stab it, giving him a glare as I thrust my fork into it. A chuckle left him, and I turned to the pieces left in the box. "Annex has grown to be a major competitor in the streaming content market, and I was part of that. The size of the company monetarily has jumped leaps and bounds from where it was a decade ago. I feel proud that I was part of that. I helped a man make his dream come to fruition."

"What about your dreams?"

His brow scrunched up as he thought about my words. "I've been going and going for so long that I'm not sure what my dreams are anymore."

"That's sad."

"What about you?" he asked.

"Oh, you know I'm passionate about numbers. I just want to keep working my way up. Maybe bump you from your position one day." I gave him a wink, which only made him laugh. "I've only been with Annex for five years, but I know it's grown a ton in that time. We used to only take up one floor, and now we take up three, and we are only one satellite location. Technically Annex is a Chicago company."

"I guess in a way you can thank me for your job," he said with a chuckle.

My brow furrowed. "What do you mean?"

"It was my idea to create a financial office in Indianapolis. It was a good-sized city that wasn't too far away where rent was a hell of a lot cheaper per square foot and cost of living was less, so salaries aren't as high, but we can still pay well. Plus different taxation."

It made me curious. What if he hadn't done that? What if he'd chosen another city? Would that have had a bearing on us meeting? Would I have gone up to Chicago for New Year's Eve and met him?

How different would my life have been if it wasn't for him?

I managed to keep him out of his office for the rest of the night, and in the morning neither of us seemed to want to leave the bed. We made love, soft and sweet, and after stayed snuggled in the warmth of each other.

I ran my hand around his torso, loving the feel of his warm skin covering layers of muscle. "How do you manage to keep this with the hours you work and the food you eat?"

He chuckled. "It's more maintenance than anything. Plus, I work out every day I'm not seeing you, and those days it's just a different type of workout. And I normally am a healthy eater. Lean proteins, lots of vegetables, whole grains."

"You can get that delivered?"

"I get most of my food from the meal delivery services, not takeout. So I do get to use my kitchen some." His fingers attacked my side, making me laugh. "Let's get some breakfast."

"Sounds good."

I rolled over him, then off his side of the bed. I threw my arms up in the air when both feet hit the floor.

"And she sticks the landing!"

He chuckled behind me, and I turned as he threw his legs over the edge of the bed. Isolated against the sheets, I got a good look at his leg, the scars that littered the skin, and the small difference in musculature from one leg to the other.

I kneeled down in front of him and wrapped my hands around his calves. I could feel the difference I'd seen. His once broken leg had never regained the muscle mass of his other leg, but it was only mildly perceptible. I trailed my fingers along his scar, noticing each tiny white dot that indicated where a stitch had been placed, and there were many. He twitched and pulled his leg back and away from me.

"Oh, I'm sorry. Does it hurt?"

His lips pressed against the crown of my head. "No, but the light touch doesn't feel right. Some of the nerves never connected back together, and it makes it feel like you're rubbing sandpaper against my skin."

"I'm sorry."

"There is nothing to be sorry about. You can touch me anywhere, just when you touch me there, be a little more aggressive."

"Like this?" I asked as I put some pressure into my hand, running it along the scar. He didn't shy away or flinch.

"Just like that."

"Weird. So, just light touches?"

He nodded. "Something about it just causes an irritation."

In all my life I'd never broken a bone, which really was surprising with Carson and Wyatt. The worst injury I could remember was hitting some loose sandy gravel on the edge of the roadway while riding my bike and scraping up my thigh.

By mid-afternoon, we loaded back up in his car and headed home. The drive home was better than the drive down, though it still felt off somehow. Then again, it could have just been my imagination, given his earlier attitude.

"So, I have drawn out telling my parents long enough, and I don't want to do it alone," I said about halfway home.

He nodded in understanding. "I'll take the brunt of it."

"It's not that. Just...I want them to meet you anyway. And once they've met you, we can tell them about the baby."

He took my hand and drew it to his lips. "My little girl is growing fast, so we should do it soon before they figure it out just by looking at you."

A groan left me, and I looked down at my stomach. He was right. It wasn't noticeable in looser clothes, but it was obvious in more form-fitting wear. And my breasts were getting larger every day.

"Friday?"

"Friday sounds perfect."

Chapter FOURTEEN

Natasha

April

I bit at my nail as I stared at the clock.

He was late.

Dinner was a big deal—meet-the-parents kind of big deal. Oh, and telling my parents about my pregnancy and hoping they didn't ask "how did this happen?" Because I didn't want to tell them how we met. The safe explanation was that we met through work.

I took one last look at my appearance to make sure I didn't look too pregnant. My stomach was definitely sticking out more every day, but thankfully the empire waist of the dress my mother bought me for Christmas managed to flare out enough that it wasn't noticeable. However, if I twisted and the fabric got caught, it was "hello, bump."

I had reminded Richard of our dinner plans during our nightly call, but I hadn't heard from him all afternoon.

With him getting wrapped up in work last weekend, I was seriously beginning to wonder if he was coming.

Friday traffic can be a bitch, I reminded myself.

I needed him to be there, beside me. Otherwise I didn't know what I was going to do.

The anxiety came to a head and I hit the call button. It rang three times before he answered, each ring ramping me up more.

"Hello, beautiful."

"You're coming, right?" I asked, my tone a little more frantic than I meant.

"Yes, I promise."

"When?" I pressed.

"You don't believe that I've already left?" There was a playful edge to his tone, which inspired hope.

"I'm...dubious." As the weeks went by, he'd slipped more and more back into work and missed an appointment that I had set up for him to come to. It was just a checkup, but I wanted him to meet my doctor.

More than that, I wanted him to *want* to meet my doctor. To want to be an active participant in this journey with more than just words, but actions too.

All the backsliding made me cautious, as well as anxious.

"Answer the door and see for yourself."

Just then the doorbell went off and I jumped from the couch, eyes wide. "Are you here?"

"No, I have your house under surveillance."

I rolled my eyes as I walked over to the door. With my hand on the handle, I paused and stood on my tiptoes to look through the peephole. I hung up the phone and pulled the door open.

Richard stood there and he let out a sigh when he saw me, his lips pulling up into a smile. In his hand was a bouquet of colorful flowers of all varieties.

"Those are beautiful," I said.

He stepped forward and leaned down to kiss me, his arms drawing me in. I was drunk off the kiss, and the spark ignited in my chest again.

"They were so bright and happy and reminded me so much of you."

"I'm not as delicate as they are."

"Maybe not, but you are beautiful and bring me so much happiness."

My chest clenched. There was my Richard. Not the VP stuck in work mode, but the man who adored me.

I took the arrangement from him and breathed in the fresh, light floral scent. "Suck up."

He grinned and shrugged. "Maybe."

"Thank you." I stood on the tips of my toes and pulled him down to press my lips to his. Even his kisses were back to full and heady. I set the vase down on the table and moved toward the door. "Are you ready to meet my family?" I asked as I pulled on my coat.

"Family? I thought it was just your parents."

My lips formed a tight line. "Turns out my brothers are being little shits."

He blew out a breath. "I'm going to get the third degree, aren't I?"

"Yup."

He heaved a sigh. "No time like the present to get the shit beat out of me."

"They won't…er, they might not do that." I grimaced and quickly backpedaled my automatic response. It wasn't beyond imagination that Carson and Wyatt would try to intimidate Richard. They had a history of it with past boyfriends. Carson was the worst with Mike, my senior prom date. He ditched me halfway through the night and refused to talk to me again after that.

"Your change in direction does not inspire confidence."

I shrugged. "It'll be fine." I headed toward my car and stopped when I noticed Richard wasn't behind me. "What are you doing?"

"Driving."

"You don't know where we're going," I pointed out.

"You can navigate."

"I can drive, is what I can do," I argued.

"True, but how am I going to finger your pussy if you're driving?"

My mouth went slack and I blinked at him. He stepped closer, his gaze flashing to my lips, then back up to my eyes. The burning electricity of his touch zinged across my skin as he tugged me against him.

"I need a taste to get me through the night," he said. His lips ghosted mine before pressing in. After a soft few seconds he pulled back. I stretched up to follow him, ignoring that self-satisfied smirk he was showing off.

"Tease," I hissed.

He stepped back and held open the passenger side door of his Acura RDX as I slipped in. As soon as we had our seat belts on, his hand was resting on my thigh.

"Where to?"

"Take a right out of the complex."

He pulled out of the spot and once the car was shifted back into drive, his hand was again on my thigh, inching its way up.

"Determined, aren't you?" I asked as I drew in a breath when his fingers brushed against the fabric of my panties.

"I'm just happy you wore a dress. If I'd been able to get here earlier, I would have already fucked you and taken this edge off."

My hips arched as his fingers slipped beneath the fabric, brushing against my slit.

"Maybe one of us will be able to get off before dinner."

I looked over to him before slipping my arm under his and reaching across, my hand brushing against the hard ridge in his slacks.

He drew in a breath through his teeth, then plunged his fingers inside me.

I cried out, my head falling back against the headrest, hips drawing up with each thrust of his fingers.

"Touch me again, and I'm pulling over and fucking you wherever we are," he growled.

"That just makes me want to touch you more."

He pressed his palm against my clit. "You're fucking insatiable."

I drew in a gasping breath. "Says the man currently finger fucking me."

"I didn't say you were the only insatiable one."

"Left at the light," I said with a moan.

"How far is it?"

"Not far enough." I bit down on my finger as I worked myself on his hand.

"Good," he said.

"Good?" I didn't like the way he said that.

"You'll be just as desperate as I am."

"We're not fucking in my parents' house." Though I said the words, the idea turned me on, something Richard seemed to pick up on.

"Maybe the bathroom. Your childhood bedroom?"

A whimper left me. "R-right up where that s-silver car turned."

"Is that their neighborhood?" he asked.

"Y-yes." I ground hard against his hand, chasing my orgasm, praying to reach it before we arrived at their house.

Richard's hand disappeared from between my legs and a keening, desperate sound escaped my throat.

"Please," I begged, my hips undulating, body begging for him to continue.

At the stop sign, he looked around before meeting my gaze. He lifted the fingers that had been in me to his mouth, and pressed his tongue flat against them before he closed his mouth around them. A contented moan resonated in his chest.

"Which way?"

My brow furrowed as I stared at him. He moved his gaze forward, and I followed.

"Right," I said. "Jerk."

A chuckle left him. "Now we're in the same state."

"I was so close."

"Maybe I will get to fuck you in your bedroom."

"You suck," I said, sticking my lower lip out as far as I could.

A groan left him and he squeezed my thigh. "Yeah, you're going to suck my cock in your childhood bedroom."

"Left." If I pulled his cock out, could I get him off before we made it up the driveway?

"It's your fault," he said, but I refused to take the bait.

"Third house on the right."

He quirked a brow at me. "Ignoring me now?"

"I'm sorry, I don't negotiate with terrorists," I said, refusing to even look at him.

"Terrorist?" he asked in surprise.

"You just terrorized my pussy."

"I scared your pussy? I'm really going to have to apologize to it then."

I nodded in agreement. "You put it in extreme distress and failed to calm it down. Now it's in a heightened state of defense."

"Fuck, does that mean you're going to be tighter?"

I turned to look at him. "What?"

"Defense? Try and keep my cock out?"

My heart sped up. Could I give him a tour and get us both off in a few short minutes? Tempting.

"You're incorrigible." I shook my head as we pulled into the driveway. "Shit." I pulled down the vanity mirror and gave myself the once-over, then pulled my dress back down. As I looked down all I could see was the perfect round bulge my body had acquired. I needed to make certain my stomach was hidden by the table when I sat down.

"Beautiful as always."

I turned in the seat. "A couple of things before we go in. One, we met at work."

He quirked a brow. "We did, did we?"

"Yes. My parents don't need to know how we really met and got pregnant. And it's technically not a lie. We did find each other again at work."

He nodded in agreement. "So we met before New Year's Eve."

"Last thing I need is my grandmother finding out we fucked the night we met and I got pregnant."

"Please tell me your grandmother isn't here as well."

"No, but you'll meet her one day, and unless you want her calling me a hussy, tramp, or whore—because that's what all unwed mothers are—you'll stick to this slightly altered origin story."

His lips formed a thin line. "Your grandmother sounds like a peach."

I rolled my eyes. "Granny is one of a kind. She's ninety-four and not a day past nineteen twenties thinking."

"Sounds familiar," he grumbled. "Just to make sure I have this all correct, the timeline is all the same, just that we met earlier."

"Yes. And started dating, but it was still early in the relationship so I didn't tell them that's why I wanted to go to Chicago for New Year's."

He blew out a breath. "I don't like lying to your parents, but if this is going to make our situation easier to swallow, I'm in."

"Thank you." I glanced to the house and hissed when I saw the curtain swing back into place. "We better go in."

We exited the car, and I led the way up the steps and was turning the handle when the door flew open and my mother stood there with a manic grin on her face. "Nat!" She pulled me in for a tight squeeze, then pulled back. She brushed the hair back from my face. "Are you all right, baby?"

I nodded. "I'm fine, Mom." I stepped aside to give Mom the full force that was Richard and was pleased at her stunned reaction. It also took the heat off me. "Mom, this is my boyfriend, Richard. Richard, my mom, Tabitha."

Richard stepped forward and held out his hand. "It's a pleasure to meet you, Tabitha."

"Likewise."

Hooked.

The way she held one hand to her chest and the starstruck look in her eyes told me she was under his spell. Not that it was a surprise.

"Your father is in the kitchen finishing up dinner," Mom said in an airy tone, her eyes not straying from Richard.

"Dad, Mom's making googly eyes at my boyfriend!" I called out, and that broke her from her trance.

"Natty!" She swatted at my arm, her face lighting up to a shade of beet red.

"Leave the man alone, Tabby-cat!" my dad called from the kitchen.

I reached out for Richard's hand and pulled at it, guiding him down the hall and into the kitchen. The closer we got, the stronger the smell of steak became, and I began salivating.

"That smells so good, Dad," I said with an appreciative groan. My stomach gave a rumble of agreement.

"Thanks, Natty."

Richard leaned in and whispered in my ear. "Natty?"

I rolled my eyes. "Fucktard number one's fault. He called me bratty Natty, and Natty stuck."

Dad looked up from the grill on the gas stove, eyes wide at the sight of Richard. "You must be the new guy."

"Dad," I groaned.

"Hopefully one day you'll refer to me as the old guy or the only guy, or my daughter's boyfriend."

Dad paused for a second, looked Richard over, nodded, then held out his hand. "Nice to meet you. I'm Greg."

"Richard," he said as he shook my dad's hand.

There was a sudden commotion at the front door, and I let out a groan.

"You can't do that."

"Says who?"

"Everyone, you little shit."

"Little shit? Take that back, fucker."

This was followed by the sound of what could be headlocks, possible stomach punching, and general horsing around. I pursed my lips and looked up at Richard, whose gaze was glued to the entrance to the kitchen.

"Boys, settle down!" Dad called.

"Not until he says I'm right!" Wyatt yelled.

"Fuck you, shit stain!" Carson growled.

A crash, followed by a couple of moans, and I walked into the foyer, my arms crossed over my chest. They were a mass of limbs and body parts on the tile floor. It was hard to tell where one man ended and the other began.

"We have a guest. Great impression, fucktards."

"Hey, Nat," Carson said with a grin from under Wyatt's arm.

"Nat, help me take him down," Wyatt begged as he pulled at Carson's arm.

"You're on your own. Car, there's an open, left arm."

"Thanks."

A knuckle into some ribs and the fight was over. Two grown men lay spread out, trying to catch their breaths.

"You don't love me, Nat," Wyatt said with a pout.

I shook my head at the two of them. "Glad to see you two are on your best behavior."

Wyatt jumped to his feet and looked to the man behind me. "Is this him?"

"You look familiar," Carson said. Standing beside one another, it was easy to tell they were brothers. Both ended up almost a full foot taller than me, as I inherited my grandmother's short stature. Wyatt's brown hair was the same shade as mine, but his highlights were due to the sun and not the chemical process I used. Carson had Dad's green eyes, and they both had the same nose, lips, and eyebrows. With the exception of Carson's slightly bent nose from when I accidentally broke it when I was a moody fourteen-year-old, their features were near identical.

"Oh shit, dude," Wyatt said as he slapped Carson in the abdomen. "Remember that show we watched last night, the one with football's worst injuries?"

"Yeah?"

"That's number twenty-three—Rick Bennett. The guy who got tackled and you could see his leg snap."

"Oh, shit!" Carson jumped back and looked Richard up and then down. "What the hell are you doing with her?"

In one second I went from beaming with pride to ready to shove my older brother into a shallow grave. "I may be small, but I can still slap the shit out of you. Speaking of, where is Hannah? She's usually down to help gang up on you."

"You're not dragging my wife into it today."

"All right, enough," Mom said as she pulled each of the boys in for a hug. "Dinner is ready."

I followed Mom, and from behind me I could hear Wyatt asking Richard about his injury.

"It was a fluke accident," Richard said. "Just landed wrong. It could have happened to anyone."

"What happened?" Dad asked, clueing into the conversation.

"Rick was a football player," Carson answered.

Dad's brows shot up. He was a major football fan. "Really? Who did you play for?"

"Clemson."

"A Clemson grad? Nice catch, Natty." Dad winked at me, and it took a lot to not roll my eyes at him.

The conversation turned to Richard's injuries and the end of his football career. I already knew about it, but somehow it hurt more to hear about it again. I wasn't sure if it was because of the feelings I'd developed, or the egging on from Carson and Wyatt for more information, but I found myself taking hold of his hand and squeezing.

"That sounds rough," Dad said with a shake of his head. "You seem to be doing well for yourself. I haven't heard how you two met."

"We met at Annex. Richard is the VP of Finance," I said as I cut into my steak. Perfect medium. Again, my father was the grill master.

"I thought you lived in Chicago," Dad said with a furrow of his brow as he took the container of butter from Carson.

We didn't have family meals very often anymore, but when we did, there was still that symphony of things moving around the table from when we all lived under the same roof.

"I do. Our executive campus is in Chicago."

"Is he your boss, Natasha?" Mom asked. She was leaning forward, almost desperate to be let in on some secret.

"Technically, yes. I didn't know he was the VP when we met, though."

"You didn't meet at the office, then?"

My brow scrunched and I shook my head. Things were getting twisted.

"We met by accident outside of the office, and then found out we worked for the same company," Richard said, saving the day.

I squeezed his hand again, already thinking of an appropriate thank you. Maybe that romp in my childhood bedroom was on the table.

"Since then, we've been working on a budget proposal and spending the weekends together," I said.

"So that's why you've been so unavailable," Mom said with a grumble. She turned to give Richard a disapproving "you are keeping my daughter from me look" but as soon as her gaze landed on him, she was a puddle of goo again. I totally understood the reaction—it was mine every time I looked at him.

"We have something we wanted to tell you about," I said, my voice steadier than I felt. Reaching down to my purse, I pulled out the ultrasound picture, then placed it on the center of the table. "Congratulations, you're going to be grandparents."

My mom's fork slipped from her fingers and clattered against the ceramic plate below. The entire table was silent, even Carson and Wyatt as they looked between our parents for a reaction.

The good-natured smile fell from my father's face, and his features seemed to oscillate between disappointment, anger, happiness, and what I could only describe as his what-the-fuck expression.

"You're pregnant?" Mom asked in a whisper.

"You just met," Dad argued.

"Damn, man," Wyatt said as he placed a hand on Richard's shoulder. "You're lucky you're here and part of her life, or I'd come hunt you down in Chicago with my bat."

"And I'd bring the plastic and shovel," Carson added.

"It wasn't planned, obviously. We're both nervous, but that doesn't mean we aren't happy."

"You just met!" Dad yelled, his fists slamming on the table before he pinched the bridge of his nose. "You're on such a great path in your career. How could you be so irresponsible, Natasha?"

The harshness of his words stung, and tears began to fill my eyes.

"Yes, it's early," Richard said, his jaw tightly set. "Yes, we made a poor decision in the heat of the moment. But this—" he pointed to the ultrasound "—this is our future, and yours. We love our future, and we hope you will, too."

I couldn't help but stare at Richard as he talked. It was an instantaneous move to take his face in my hands and pull him down for a kiss.

"Thank you," I whispered as I pulled back.

He put his hand on mine, keeping it on his cheek before turning his head and placing a kiss on my palm.

"Greg, Natasha and I are both responsible individuals," Richard said, not wavering from my father's stare. "Our child will be cared for and loved and want for nothing. While still young, as you pointed out, we are in a committed relationship."

My father nodded. "I'm sorry, pumpkin." He reached across the table for my hand. "I let the shock get the best of me and said things I shouldn't have."

"Thank you, Daddy."

"Well, on that note…" Carson said, gaining attention. "The reason Hannah isn't here is because, well, morning sickness."

Mom's eyes grew wide, and my head whipped over to my brother.

"Thunder stealer," I said with a glare.

He held up his hands. "We were going to tell everyone tonight, sis. You just beat me to the punch."

Mom sniffed before standing and coming around the table. Her arms wrapped tightly around me, then grabbed Carson.

"I'm going to be a grandma!"

Dad appeared beside me and pulled me in for a hug, and in that moment I forgave him for his outburst.

"Love you, bug," he said.

"Love you, too, Daddy."

He turned to Richard and held out his hand. "Thanks for helping me pull my head from my ass."

At that, Richard chuckled and shook his hand. "Anytime."

Hugs continued all around, and everyone sat back down to continue the meal.

"Now all we need is Wyatt to get a girl," I said, quirking my brow at him.

"No girl is going to tie me down," he grumbled.

"You say that now, ball boy, but one day she'll catch you," Carson quipped.

One word stuck out. "She? As in a specific she?" I asked.

Wyatt glared at Carson. "I fucking told you little Miss Lie Detector would catch it."

"She's like that with everyone, not just me, huh?" Richard said.

"Off me and back to she. Who is she?"

Wyatt shook his head, his jaw locked, refusing to answer, so I turned my attention to Carson.

"He's got a super fan," he revealed.

"Stalker?"

"No, but she lives in the same complex as me, and I bump into her *everywhere*. It really is all coincidence, though it doesn't seem like it."

"And you haven't asked her out because?" I pressed.

"She isn't my type," he grumbled in response, refusing to look at anything but his plate.

"Lies," Carson whispered.

"Shut up!" Wyatt groaned before tossing a roll at Carson's head.

Carson laughed but didn't let up. "She's chubby, and pretty, and sweet."

I nodded in understanding. "Wyatt's kryptonite."

"You all suck." Wyatt's cheeks were bright pink, and I could tell he really did like her, despite his attempts to dissuade us.

"Just ask her out, knock her up, and I'll have three grandbabies on the way," Mom said with a smile.

"Mom!" Wyatt whined.

"And when are my first two babies coming?" she asked, completely ignoring her youngest child.

Mom was on cloud nine. I was certain she was itching to go shopping and load up on baby stuff. She'd probably already imagined how she'd turn one of the bedrooms upstairs into a nursery, decorations and all.

"Hannah is due October sixth," Carson said at the same time I answered, "September twenty-third."

"Oh, we could do dual baby showers!" Mom cried.

I caught the roll of Dad's eyes before he shook his head, but the smile on his face said he expected the response from her.

Two hours later, we were back in my apartment and I was ready to fall into bed. Richard stepped up behind me and wrapped his arms around me and pulled me close. "I'm glad we got that over with."

"Me, too."

"How did they take it compared to how you thought?"

"About the same, actually. The shock, a dash of disappointment, and then happiness. Wasn't expecting Carson's announcement, though."

"Your brothers are fun," he said with a chuckle.

I rolled my eyes. He had no idea that was them in good behavior mode. "They're holy terrors."

"Maybe for you. It's obvious how much they love you."

"Okay, somewhat lovable little shits." I really did love their stupid asses.

"You're hysterical with them. Susie and I were never as close as you three are."

"Why not?"

He shrugged. "I was into sports, she was into Barbie."

"I was stomping through creeks with frick and frack. I guess I was a bit of a tomboy thanks to them."

He sat on the edge of the bed and pulled me closer, his eyes on my bump. "Baby girl, you can play with whatever you want. If you're into Transformers, that's awesome. If dress-up is your thing, I'll have tea parties with you."

I smiled down at him and brushed my fingers through his hair. "What if your son wants to play dress-up?"

He tilted his head back and ran his hands over my stomach. "Let him. I'm not going to pigeonhole our child into some societal construct of what a boy or girl should do or be."

It felt good to hear him say that, but it also hurt, because I could tell they were words born out of experience. Maybe he and his sister weren't close because of those views. Maybe they weren't allowed to be because boys weren't supposed to have feelings or some archaic view like that.

The way he clung to me, I realized Richard had more darkness in him than just from the pain from his divorce.

Chapter FIFTEEN

Richard

For the past week Natasha helped me to smooth out and perfect the budget analysis, and I was quite impressed with her work. She had it more streamlined than I'd been able accomplish on my own in the past.

We both had stayed up late, talking on the phone, emailing back and forth in the final week, until everything was just right. I knew it took a toll on her, and I was ready to free her for an early weekend, to pamper her a little.

And to share the excitement of a job well done.

The walls built to protect myself from Natasha did nothing to stifle the deep-seated desire I had for her. Natasha had worked her way into my bloodstream and had become a drug my body needed regular doses of to survive.

Meeting her family only highlighted how dysfunctional my family was. Susie and I weren't close like that because she was a girl and I was a boy. Girls cooked and cleaned and sewed and played with dolls, while boys did hard chores outside, played sports, and made money.

I had a paper route by eight, and at thirteen I was working in the fields during the summer baling hay. We didn't live in the city, but in a small town, and we hated every day of it. That was the only link Susie and I had at the time.

There was little affection, and absolutely no coddling allowed by our father. Maybe that's why I fell so hard for Desiree when we met. She was affectionate and warm and loved football and allowed me to do things that had otherwise been frowned upon because I was a boy.

My father would have hated that I met Natasha dancing. That I showered her with kisses and was always looking for a way to touch her, to be close to her. That I allowed her to make decisions and asked her opinion.

Susie was opinionated, and that drove our father crazy. Once she was out of the house, she was like me—able to grow as a person and not a shadow of our parents' outdated ideas.

I didn't want that sort of stilted nurturing for our children, and no matter how thick the walls were around me, I couldn't stop envisioning our future.

I locked down my emotions during the week, but the moment I saw her, that need came spilling out.

I wrapped my arms around her waist, dipping my head into her neck. A groan left me as I breathed her in.

"You are the perfect medicine for a long week."

A giggle left her as I looked around the cubicles surrounding hers and the wide-eyed stares that were aimed at us. "Well, my week isn't over."

"Yes, it is," I said. I needed it to be.

She turned in my arms. "You're making a scene."

"I don't care." Fuck them all. She was mine, and everyone would know it. They were both mine.

She ran her hands against my chest. "Why are you so desperate?"

"Because I missed you." But that was only the surface.

"Well, you're going to have to miss me for a few more hours. I have work to get done," she said as she stepped away.

I took hold of her hand and tugged her back. "I bet I can clear it with your boss."

"Oh, Richard, I didn't realize you were coming in today," Marjorie said with a strained smile.

My jaw ticked as I stared at her. "Hello, Marjorie."

Her gaze bounced between us, then down to our joined hands. Her mouth snapped shut, jaw ticking, a struggle of a forced smile on her lips.

The growing tension was palpable, and Natasha tried to pull her hand from mine but I kept a firm grip. I wanted the crap with this woman over and in the open, because I was certain words were about to fly from her mouth that I would make her regret.

From what Nat said, Marjorie had never liked her. I knew for a fact she didn't like Nina either. How had this woman never understood that *she* was the problem?

"Hey, Richard," Jenna said, stepping forward and holding her hand up for a high five.

I slapped her hand. "Jenna. How's Brent?"

"Good. What's going on here?"

I smiled at her. "I came to see my girls."

Natasha rolled her eyes, a smile playing on her lips. "You don't know it's a girl."

"Don't doubt me," I said with a smirk. I reached out and placed my hand on her bump, anxiously waiting for the day she kicked back. "Baby Girl Bennett. I'm telling you."

Marjorie's jaw was slack as she looked at us. "I knew you couldn't have gotten that promotion without help," she spat.

Natasha froze, her gaze locked on Marjorie. "Excuse me?"

"I suspected you were screwing your way up the corporate ladder, but now I know." Marjorie's face was screwed up and red with anger.

"Of course you would think that," Natasha said sourly.

"Marjorie, back down before I file a grievance with HR," I growled. Her jealous accusation made my blood boil.

Marjorie blanched. "Why?"

My brows shot up. Did she really think her words were

acceptable? Not in any business. How had someone so inept with people become a manager? I needed to look into that when I got home.

"Why? Because you just insinuated that my girlfriend was fucking her way up. Our relationship is not a topic of your concern."

"Company policy states—"

Oh, fuck that!

"Do not recite company policy to *me*." I could barely contain the anger that wanted to explode forth. "I've read her employee file, I know how she was promoted, and it was due to hard work and knowledge, and it happened before we met. What is your problem? Why do you feel the need to police everything going on in this office? Do you get off on putting others down? On feeling superior? Get off your fucking high horse or I will pull you off. You do not hold the company's interest in mind, only your own, and you refuse to be a team player, singling yourself out. You don't rule here, *I do*."

Natasha's fingers wove with mine, her other arm wrapped around my bicep.

Enough. I'd had enough of Marjorie's attitude, and I would not allow her to talk about Natasha that way.

Marjorie blinked at me, wetness filling her eyes. "You're right, sir. I'm sorry. I will go reflect on my actions and strive to be a better employee."

"So there's that vicious VP I've heard so much about," Jenna said as we watched Marjorie walk away.

"I'm not going to fucking apologize for hurting her feelings."

"Who said you had to?" Jenna asked.

Natasha let my hand go and stepped forward. In my periphery, I watched her falter and lean against a nearby desk for support.

"Are you okay?" I asked as I rushed to her side, my arms around her to support her weight.

"Yeah," she said as she rested her head on my chest. "I just got dizzy all of a sudden."

"Sit down." I directed her to a nearby chair, then grabbed another one for myself.

"Thank you," she said.

I took hold of her chin to look at her eyes for anything that seemed off. "Does this happen often?" There was one day a few weeks ago that she was shaking, but I didn't remember her being dizzy.

She shook her head. "A few times."

"Have you told your doctor about it?" I asked.

A nod that time. "Dizziness is another side effect of pregnancy. Just like the morning sickness."

"Can I take you home now?" I asked, desperate to get her somewhere she could lie down.

She nodded, and I helped her to stand.

I'd made on-the-sly arrangements for Natasha to carpool with Jenna, making it easier for me to steal her away. That way when we left, all she had to do was grab her bag and we were off.

"How did it go?" she asked as we drove out of the parking lot.

We hadn't talked about my blowup at Marjorie, and that was fine by me, but I also hadn't gotten to tell her how the meeting went. I wished she could have been there with me, but I made sure to give her credit, especially to her direct manager.

We'd worked so many hours on the budget proposal, and in the end found most items to be a worthy gamble. It was whether or not Michael and the other executives agreed.

"They were very pleased with *our* recommendations."

A smile lit up her face. "Really?"

I nodded. "Really. So, you may be volunteered to help out the VP more in the future."

"Oh, not him again."

A chuckle left me. "Really? You're going to do me like that?"

"No, not you," she said, taking my hand in hers. "But the VP can be a real pain in my ass."

A groan left me at the image her words conjured. "Don't talk to me like that."

"Like what?" she asked.

"Oh, baby, I'd love to be a real pain in your ass."

She rolled her eyes and shook her head. "What's for dinner?"

"Whatever you want."

"Hibachi."

We'd passed the exits for the interstate, so I had to take the surface streets, including some unusual shortcuts through neighborhoods.

She let out a sigh. "I've always loved this neighborhood."

"Really? Why?" I asked. I'd lived in the city for so long, in apartments and condos, and in rural areas before that. I'd never really lived in the quintessential neighborhood.

"The houses have that traditional feel. Homey feel. There are always kids riding bikes, running around lawns. The houses are large and well taken care of with large lots."

"Is that what you want?" I asked, curious what her ideal home was.

She nodded. "Nice big kitchen with a huge island and double ovens. A screened in porch. Large, but not too large, master bedroom with a spa-like bathroom."

"How many bedrooms?"

She pursed her lips, and if I hadn't been driving I would have leaned over and bit her succulent lower lip.

"Four. And a designated office somewhere in the house. A basement for a man cave or movie room, maybe a pool table. Hardwood floors for easier cleaning."

"Sounds like you've thought a lot about it," I said, making sure I took mental note of the things she mentioned. Maybe one day we could move into the suburbs of Chicago. The commute would be hell, but I wanted to give her that dream.

"Not exactly, but I've kept a mental list of wishes. One day." She placed her hand on her bump and began brushing her hand up and down.

One day, indeed. I would make sure of it.

Chapter SIXTEEN

Natasha

When Richard asked if there was anything I wanted to do over the weekend, there was one thing I desperately needed to do. Between work and baby naps, I'd been able to accomplish zilch in the shopping department, and didn't have many clothes that could fit anymore. Baby Bump Bennett was getting bigger every week, and I was down to dresses and yoga pants.

"This store is the devil," I said to Richard as we walked through the automatic doors.

"Why is that?" he asked, his brow furrowed. "They're one of the largest retailers in the country."

"Because you go in for one five-dollar item and come out with nearly two hundred dollars' worth of stuff."

He shook his head. "That's called a lack of self-control."

"Uh-huh, just watch."

I grabbed a cart and perused the dollar bin section as we walked past. There were a few things I needed, and I made a straight line for the undergarments section. Richard's eyes popped wide when I stopped in an aisle full of bras.

"Let me buy you lingerie from somewhere better than this," he whispered in my ear.

I rolled my eyes and shook my head. "You do that, then, but I'm looking for everyday wear. My breasts keep growing—"

"Oh, I've noticed," Richard interrupted me with a smirk.

"Anyway, I need a couple new bras." A couple bralettes caught my eye and I immediately searched for a few I liked, then threw them in the basket. Those would be great. Less restrictive and still giving me some support. While probably not office attire, they would be comfortable outside of work. Thankfully, the tenderness had gotten better.

We moved to the maternity section, and I scoured the rack for work-appropriate clothes. I could still wear some stuff, but anything with a button closure was a no-go. Shirts, sweaters, dresses, jeans—it all went into the cart. At least the weather was starting to warm so I didn't need to add a coat to the list.

"You aren't going to try any of that on?" Richard asked as we stepped back into the walkway and away from the dressing room.

"No."

"Why not?"

I leaned in closer, double checking there was nobody in earshot before whispering. "Because if I go in there, you'll want to follow me, and I just know seconds after you'd have your cock inside me."

A groan left him, and he stepped behind me. His lips ghosted my ear as his hips pressed into mine. "Who, me? I would never."

I bent my neck to give him better access. "Sure you wouldn't. Just like you would never do such a thing in a restaurant bathroom or at a huge New Year's Eve party in front of a window."

"Wasn't me."

A giggle left me. This was the version of him I loved. He was playful and sweet and caring. "Well, if it wasn't you, I don't know whose baby this is."

"Oh, that baby's mine." He nipped at my neck, his hand laying protectively over my bump.

"You are such an exhibitionist."

"Says the woman who had me fuck her in front of a window with no shade."

The baby section caught my eye, and I veered toward it.

"And look at the trouble that got me in," I said jokingly as I pointed down to my stomach.

Richard placed his hands on my stomach and squatted down. "Shh, Mommy doesn't mean it like that. You're not going to be trouble at all, are you, my angel?"

I smiled and shook my head, then looked at all the stuff in the aisle. There were so many...*things*. None of my close friends had kids, and I hadn't babysat an actual baby in well over a decade, so my knowledge of what most of it was equated to near nothing. Instead, I moved past all the various items into something I did know—clothes.

"Aww," I squealed and pulled a onesie from the rack. "Look."

"Mommy's dapper dude," Richard read it off. He chuckled, then pulled another from the rack. "Or the more accurate, 'Daddy's little princess.'"

A giggle left me. "You're too much."

"I'm just saying."

"And so am I."

"Nat?" someone called.

I turned to find my brother's wife standing a few feet behind me at the end of the row. "Hannah!" I stepped over and threw my arms around her. "How are you?"

"I'm good, how are you?"

"Doing great."

Her eyes glanced over to Richard, and I took his hand. "Richard, this is my sister-in-law Hannah. Hannah, this is my boyfriend, Richard."

"Ah, so you're the infamous Richard I've heard so much about."

Richard held out his hand. "All good, I hope."

"Eh, just how you got my little sis knocked up on what I'm guessing was a first date."

"Carson!" I cried out. He appeared suddenly beside me. "You scared the crap out of me."

"Is it true?" Hannah asked.

The blood rushed to my face, and I looked from Carson to Richard. "What are you talking about?"

"Oh, come on." Carson rolled his eyes and held out his hand for Richard. "It was a nice save."

"I'm sure I don't know what you're talking about," Richard said in his most diplomatic tone.

"Little Natty isn't the only observant one. She got flustered, but you saved it."

"Do you think anyone else caught it?" I asked.

He shook his head. "Nah, but it was just the timeline that was off, right?"

I nodded. "We met on New Year's Eve, and I found out he was my boss on Valentine's Day. And if you tell Mom or Dad or Wyatt, I will hurt you so bad."

He held his hands up. "Not me, I swear."

"Why not Wyatt?" Richard asked.

Hannah laughed hard in response. "Oh, sorry. You don't know him very well yet, but Wyatt can't keep a secret for anything."

Carson leaned in closer. "He finally asked her out."

"No," I said in wide-eyed shock.

"If he's a professional baseball player, doesn't he have the confidence to talk to a woman?" Richard asked.

I shook my head. "Women? Yes. One that he has interest in for more than sex? He's a complete disaster."

"Girls he likes turn him into this shy, introverted nerd that has never gotten laid," Carson elaborated in a way only a brother could.

"Once he has them, though, he's back to normal," I added.

"So are you here to baby shop?" Hannah grinned at me, eyeing my bump.

I returned the bump eyeing. "You?"

"Yes, but I'm seriously about to break into this box of cookies."

I stared down at the box in her hand. "If you do, you better share."

She giggled and broke open the box, pulled out a sleeve, then handed the box to Carson. "Babe, go pay for this."

"And get me a water!" I called after him.

Hannah's eyes lit up. "And a Diet Coke!"

"Rick? Anything while I'm being an errand boy?" Carson asked as he walked backward away from us.

Richard waved him off. "I'm fine, thanks."

"How are you feeling?" Hannah asked as she bit into her second cookie.

"Better," I said with a relieved sigh. "I literally fell asleep at work the other week and didn't wake until my head slipped and slammed into the desk."

"Ouch. You didn't tell me that," Richard said before leaning forward and pressing his lips to my forehead.

"Yeah, tell my boss I fell asleep at my desk," I said with a jab of my elbow. "It was more out of embarrassment."

"And the vomit. A whole week without throwing up, thank you," Hannah said in a reverent tone.

"I lucked out there. My morning sickness was mild, so it was only a couple times a week."

Carson returned with our drinks and the rest of the box of cookies, which was good because Hannah and I had nearly polished off the first sleeve.

Richard's phone went off, and he pulled it from his jacket. He grimaced as he looked at the screen. "I'll be right back," he said before stepping away.

And Mr. VP was back. I let out a sigh, praying to the heavens his good mood would still be there when he returned.

"He's handsome," Hannah said with a wink.

"Oh, trust me, I am well aware." I turned and eyed his backside. His very muscular backside.

"How's it going with you two?" Hannah asked, drawing my

attention and handing over another cookie. "Must have been a shocker to him, but he seems excited."

"Things are great. Work is getting busy, hence the phone call. And he has been nothing but happy about the baby."

Hannah squeezed my hand. "That is so good. Okay, I've been meaning to call you. I've been going to this pregnancy yoga class on Tuesday nights. You should come."

"That would be great." It really would be. Truth was, I needed to spend more time on the pregnancy stuff and baby prep. My days were filled with work, and my weekends were filled with Richard. And the evenings were filled with naps and chapters of my what-to-expect books. I'd scanned a few blogs on my phone, and had a baby room Pinterest board going.

Having Hannah to talk to, someone who was going through the same thing as me only a week or two behind, would be great.

"All right, cookie monster," Carson said as he pulled his wife close. I kept a close watch on the cookies, but he was a good boy and didn't dare try and take them from her. "We've got lunch with your parents in a few minutes."

"Oh! I almost forgot." She turned back to me. "I'll text you, and we can meet up on Tuesday. Maybe get a bite after."

"Perfect." I gave them both a hug.

Carson called out across the store to Richard and gave him a wave before they headed toward checkout.

"Sorry about that," Richard said when he returned a few seconds later. He picked up the Daddy's little princess onesie and put it in the cart. "We are getting this."

"We won't know until June if it's a girl or boy."

He shook his head. "I'm buying it."

I stood up on the tips of my toes and pressed my lips to his cheek. "You're adorable."

We continued around the baby section and Richard found the plush animals. He pulled a bear from the shelf. "She has to have a teddy bear."

There was nothing flashy about the bear. It was a standard bear, but the way he was looking at it made my chest clench.

"I like that one," I said.

"I had one a lot like this as a kid," he said, running his hand over the soft fabric.

"So, we've told my parents. When are we telling yours?" I asked. They were the only ones left.

He froze, his grip tightening on the bear.

"What is it?" I asked, placing my hand on his.

"My father has…ideas about how men and women should behave. He's very gender-role oriented."

"Okay."

"He'll ask when you're quitting your job. When you're moving in. When are we getting married? What's the best dish you cook? How you're going to take care of me. Questions that I don't have answers to and ones that I don't agree with. I don't want you to meet him and think that is what I want from you."

His jaw twitched, and I cupped his cheek, bringing his eyes to mine. "It's okay. I know."

"Desiree refused to be around him after we got married, and when we got divorced he said it was because I didn't enforce my male rights."

My stomach dropped. "Male rights?"

He nodded. "It's just as it sounds. He's my father, but I don't want you anywhere near him."

"What about your mom?" I asked.

He swallowed hard. "She falls right in line, because that's how she was raised."

"And Susie?"

He made a small huffing sound. "We can call her tonight."

Chapter SEVENTEEN

Natasha

Early May

It was becoming a thing. An indecent, attention-seeking whore of a thing. As needy as a drug addict searching for their next hit.

And when it struck it destroyed all the happiness in my heart, especially when Richard was already a day late. I'd expected him on Friday night, like usual, but work had its hooks in him, unrelenting.

I no longer felt comfortable telling him everything that was going on because he stopped being as open in conversation.

"Shit blew up, and I'm sitting here volleying emails with my bag sitting next to me trying not to break my laptop," Richard said. The edge in his voice told me how pissed he was without the matching words.

"Well, crap." I rubbed at the space between my eyes in an attempt to ward off the headache that was coming on, mostly due to the agitation of work taking over again.

Work was the one thing that demanded his attention, that snapped its non-existent fingers and made him jump. I couldn't even get him to come with me to a doctor's appointment, but one phone call or email and work had his undivided attention.

I wished I was as important to him.

"I'm sorry. I was literally walking out the door when my phone rang, and now I'm putting out fires."

"I understand." I almost told him it was okay, but that would have been a lie. It wasn't okay. It was tiring, and I was beginning to feel my importance slipping.

"I'll get there as soon as I can."

"You should get moving then. Keep me updated." I tried to hide my disappointment, but I could feel it bleeding out in my words.

"I will. Talk to you soon."

"Bye." I hung up the phone and stared down at my bump. "What do you want to do today, kiddo?" There was a soft flutter inside me in answer.

I hadn't even gotten to tell Richard that the baby was moving. I thought it was gas at first, but when I told my doctor yesterday, she said the baby had quickened. I also hadn't gotten to tell him what else the doctor talked about during my checkup.

I ran my hand down my bump and flexed my toes against the carpet as I let out a sigh, noticing the swelling in my toes.

It wasn't even nine in the morning. What was I going to do with myself? For months, my free weekends were spent with Richard, and it was the first time since February I was without his presence for a few hours. I wasn't counting the times he was working when we were together, because he was with me.

"Want to see what Auntie Jenna is doing?" I asked my bump. Another flutter, and I took that as my answer.

What are you doing?—Nat

In seconds my phone buzzed with a reply. **Stuffing my face with dorayaki—Jenna**

Come over?—Nat

Be there in two—Jenna

I moved to my front door and swung it open. The air was cool on my skin, and I wrapped my cardigan tighter around me.

Across the parking lot, Jenna's door swung open and she headed over in her purple pug pajama pants, slippers, robe, and a plate full of dorayaki, one hanging from her mouth.

"Looking good, hot stuff!" I called out.

She held her arms out and did a little turn with a shake of her hips. When she got close enough I took the plate from her, enabling her to finish biting into the one in her mouth.

"Thanks."

"Did your mom make them?" I asked as I set them down on the coffee table. Dorayaki were basically sweet bean paste between two pancakes, but there was just something about them. I'd had them from other sources, but none were as good as Mamma Okada's. She said it was all the love she poured into them, but I had a feeling the answer was actually sugar.

She nodded. "She made extra for you."

"Uh-huh, and if I hadn't texted, would I have seen any of them?"

She shrugged. "If any survived the weekend."

I threw my arms around her. "Fuck, I've missed you," I said into Jenna's hair as I squeezed her tightly.

She pulled me tighter. "Ditto."

"I feel like we're disconnected in a way." It was a feeling I hated. She was the one person I told everything too, and there was so much I hadn't told her lately.

We sat down on the couch and I grabbed one of the dorayaki, a small moan leaving me as I took a bite.

"Even though we see each other every day, yeah, I get that."

"I'm blaming it on the men in our lives." And it was true. We were both spending our free time with them.

At the mention of men, Jenna's eyes went glassy and the corner of her mouth tipped up.

My eyes widened as I watched the transformation. "Wipe that look off your face. You're scaring me."

"I'm sorry. I can't help it."

"What has got you making that creepy-ass smile?" She really was freaking me out a little bit.

"Love."

I blinked at her. In the years I'd know her, Jenna liked guys, even really liked some boyfriends, but the dreamy look and the word she uttered seemed out of place. "Love? Really?"

She bit down on her bottom lip and smiled. "Brent told me last night that he loved me, and it wasn't when he was fucking me."

I worked a brow at her. "Is that normal?"

She nodded. "Both Taka and Ben did that."

"How did Brent say it?"

She let out a dreamy sigh and flopped down on the couch next to me. "It was warm last night, like 'yes, spring is finally here' so we went for a walk along the river. Just walking, hand in hand when he stopped. He leaned down to kiss me and just said it. Bam! There it was."

"And what did you do?"

"What else? I jumped him. I mean, the guy is a foot and a half taller than me. Hearing him say it, though…" she trailed off and sighed. "Yeah, I've got it bad for him. Like super bad. Like I can see marrying him, kind of love."

"Oh, Jenna, I'm so happy for you." I really was. She was a little wild and crazy, but Jenna was my person, and all I wanted was for her to find happiness.

"Brent, well, he's the first non-Asian guy I've dated that really seems to like me for me and not as some stereotypical geisha fantasy or manga character."

"Aww, that…I just…" And cue the tears.

Jenna leaned forward and wrapped her arms around me. "It's okay, hormones," she said as she petted my head. "Are you hungry? Do I need to feed the momma?"

"It's not that," I sniffed. "This stupidness started happening. I'm just so happy to see you so happy. Brent is a good guy and I've seen the way he looks at you like you're his whole world."

She smiled at me. "Turns out New Year's Eve was quite a night for both of us."

I nodded. "You know, with Brent's towering height, your kids might end up a midrange height."

She held her hands up. "Whoa, who said anything about kids? We're not there yet."

"Neither was I," I said as I pointed to my growing bump. "One time is all it takes."

"I still can't believe it happened." She leaned down and made cooing sounds at my belly while petting me.

I just laughed. "Me either. But, I just look at it as my destiny. Maybe this was the way to get us to come together."

"Speaking of Richard, where is he?"

I blew out a breath and sank back into the cushions. "Work. Something came up. He said he's going to try and come down after."

"After?"

I swallowed hard and stared down at my belly, my hand gently rubbing. In almost three months, it wasn't the first time it happened. With all the days he cut out to see me that first month, work caught up with him and now we were paying the price.

At least that was what I told myself. I tried not to let the little negative thoughts enter, but I couldn't help it. Maybe work didn't catch up, but maybe he got caught back up in work.

I plastered a smile onto my face. "It's okay, really. He should be here by dinner."

Jenna pursed her lips, her eyes in slits, just like her favorite emoji besides the laughing one. It was a look that said, "you're full of shit and I see right through you."

"Come on," she said as she leapt from the couch.

"Where are we going?"

She tugged on my hand to help me up. "We need pedicures."

Chapter EIGHTEEN

Richard

"**S**hit," I hissed as I looked at the clock. When I last glanced to the lower right of the screen, the morning sun was bouncing off the window from the other tower, but now the sun was streaming in the window. My blood went cold. I was supposed to put out the fires, then head to Natasha's, but at almost five in the afternoon, I began to wonder if I would still be welcome.

After a half second of thought, I picked up my phone and my heart dropped at the two text messages I'd missed.

Are you on your way?—Natasha

Please call me. I just want to know you're okay.—Natasha

The second one was an hour old.

Work had once again taken me from Natasha, and I knew someday she wouldn't be as understanding. In fact, I was pretty certain if I wanted her to open the door, because calling or texting was *not* an option at that point, groveling would be involved.

Immediately I shut down my laptop, but left it where it was. If I showed up with it, I knew I'd be a dead man. As I gathered my bag and headed down to my car, I began to formulate my apology.

On the phone the night before, she told me she'd been craving Mexican food. Right then, that was my way in.

I sped down the interstate, weaving between the unending line of trucks on I-65. There was a serious need for three lanes, and I couldn't understand why there were only two.

I called up Keenan and asked him to help me find a restaurant to get take-out from, and in short order I was able to place an order and pick it up. The drive was made in record time and included the stop.

I rushed to grab my bag and the food and headed up the sidewalk to her door and knocked.

When the door opened, I drew in a sharp breath. Her hair was up in a messy bun and she was dressed in what I knew to be her favorite comfort clothes—tank top, lounge pants, and a chenille cardigan.

If I had a tail, I was certain it would be tucked high up. Fuck. That look in her eyes tore at me. I should have left sooner. I should have pulled myself away, but in the moment it seemed so important.

More important than her.

However, looking at her, at the redness around her eyes, I began to wonder what was so important that it would keep me from her?

Natasha was like fresh air. Every time I saw her was almost like the first time all over again.

And even with all that, the thoughts crawled in. The dark ones that cornered me when I was in Chicago and far from her. They didn't want the warmth that filled my chest when I was around her. They wanted to put walls up to keep her out.

That darkness wanted walls all the way to the upper stratosphere to keep those feelings at bay.

"I brought tacos as a peace offering. With queso and salsa. And some ice cream."

She tilted her head and pursed her lips while she decided, but the rumble of her stomach gave her away. "Fine, but this will pay for your entrance in and nothing more. I'm not some booty call."

I stepped forward, confident she wasn't going to stab me, though her gaze kept me a little on edge. Leaning down, I pressed my lips to hers, but the response from her was lackluster. She was angry, and rightfully so, but I hoped the food would soften her up.

After setting my overnight bag down, I moved to the kitchen and pulled dishes down from the cabinet and began spreading the food onto the plates. She sat at the table, watching me, waiting.

I set the plate of chicken tacos on the table in front of her along with the container of queso and a bowl of chips before returning for the lime slices and sour cream, and to throw the ice cream into the freezer.

"How was your day?" I asked. Her head shot up, and she raised a brow at me.

She let out a moan at her first bite, and when she finished the first taco, she dipped a few chips in queso before answering me. And I'd learned it was in my best interest to wait for her response, especially when she was hungry.

"Aggravating. Because I was waiting for you, I was left on edge all day. Hannah wanted to go to yoga, and I said no, because you were due any minute."

"I'm so—"

"I don't want to hear that. I want to hear what was so important that you couldn't keep your promise. And I *know* what is going on at Annex, so no bullshit."

"I have obligations that you don't know about."

"Way to be vague."

With that, she stood and took her plate, tossing it into the sink before heading to the bedroom. I waited a few minutes, expecting her to come back out, but she didn't.

The gap between us grew into a larger expanse.

The next morning I woke up on the couch, my back killing me. The bedroom door was still firmly shut. I didn't even try to crawl into bed with her. I deserved to sleep on the couch.

My whole body was stiff and I ran my hands down my face. When was the last time I'd been so thoroughly in the dog house?

I wasn't even sure I could blame her.

Time and time again, I let work repeat the same hijack.

While the Mexican food the night before got me in the door, it didn't make up for work corrupting me again. Breakfast was my way to get back in her good graces enough that maybe she'd talk to me.

It was barely half past six, and I went to the bathroom, quiet not to wake her while I brushed my teeth and threw some water on my face. Afterwards I surfed multiple menus until I found something she would like. And if that didn't work for her, I ordered three other things off the menu.

I placed the order, and then quietly opened the door to the bedroom. Soft little snores alerted me to her still-sleeping state, and I snuck out the front door, making sure to take her keys so I could lock the door.

The food was due to arrive in half an hour, giving me just enough time to hit up the coffee shop. I arrived back before she woke, but the doorbell going off a few minutes later roused her.

She had a grumpy little frown on her face when she stepped out of the bedroom, her hair a mess, sticking everywhere.

I thanked the driver as I took the bags from his hand, then shut the door.

"You're still here," she said. I wasn't sure how to take it as her voice was part awe and part she devil, and I really wasn't sure which one was winning out.

"Where else would I be?"

She shrugged. "Asleep on the couch in your office?"

Ouch. That hurt, but it was a truthful hit.

I placed the bags on the table, then grabbed the cup I'd gotten for her.

"Good morning, beautiful," I said as I handed it to her.

Her brow furrowed as she took it, bringing it to her nose for a sniff. "Hot chocolate?"

I smiled at her. "Yes."

She stared down at the cup. "You got me hot chocolate?"

I nodded and picked up a bag from the table. "Chicken fried steak, eggs, gravy, and hash browns with wheat toast."

"You got me hot chocolate," she repeated, ignoring the menu I'd selected.

"Did you want coffee? I didn't think you could really have that and you ordered hot chocolate last time we were out, I just thought…" I trailed off. Had I royally fucked up? Was hot chocolate about to be thrown at me?

A tear rolled down her cheek and she sniffed. "You got me hot chocolate."

"Was that okay? If not, I can get rid of it."

She shielded the cup from me with her hands, turning it from my outstretched grasp.

"Back off."

I held my hands up and retreated backwards. "If the chicken fried steak isn't what you want, I also got pancakes and bacon, and an omelet and biscuits and sausage."

She quirked a brow at me. "Did you order the whole menu?"

"Almost."

She took a tentative sip of the hot chocolate in her hand, a moan leaving her. "So good." She stepped over to the table and took a seat.

I took that as a good sign and grabbed some plates and silverware before pulling out the containers. She greedily took a little bit of everything, and I smiled that for once this weekend I'd managed to make her happy.

"I'm sorry," I said as she stuffed a bite of pancake into her mouth. She stared at me, chewing slowly as she waited. Hot chocolate got me the in, and breakfast got me the conversation, but it was up to me to get her. "I work a lot, and I let it intrude on our time. Sometimes there are fires I just can't ignore, but I also know there are some that can wait. I need to pick better battles, because you are the most fearsome opponent I've ever dealt with."

"I'm supposed to be your partner in crime, not your battle opponent."

I nodded. "You're right."

She took another bite, her eyes never leaving mine. "And your solution is?"

My solution? I reached across the table and put my hand on hers. "The only battling I want to do with you is in the bedroom."

"Well, if you want hot make-up bedroom-battling sex, you need to turn your phone off for the rest of the day."

I blinked at her. It was a simple request, but as I stared at my phone, at the fifteen new emails since I'd left the office and three text messages, I struggled. Turning the ringer off I could do. Turning the entire thing off?

She stared at me, waiting for my decision, and as much as I hated it, there was only one answer. One way that I would return to her good graces. I held down the button and watched as the power screen flashed by, the chimes played, and then the screen was black.

Chapter
NINETEEN

Natasha

The previous weekend was a shit show. He slept on the couch that night while I cried myself to sleep. All I wanted was him. All I needed was him. To be present, to be mentally with me, to support me, but he'd checked out. The once-doting boyfriend was gone and in his stead was the VP.

In the morning he ordered breakfast and I was moved when he handed me a hot chocolate. It was a nice gesture, and I tried to find an even ground. Still, it was hard to let go of how emotional I'd become about it all.

I made him turn his phone off, and for a few hours it was just the two of us again.

However, as the days rolled on, that bitch had her claws in him again. He arrived the night before near ten, having not left until five local time. I wasn't feeling well, so we opted for a stay-in day, and I curled up on the couch while we binged a show on Annex.

I could accept the occasional bleed of work into our weekends, but the bleed was nearly all the damn time. Half of the time he was still at the office during our evening calls.

I'd offered to come up for the weekend, but he dismissed the idea, saying he needed to get away from the office and he didn't want me driving. I wasn't sure about the driving part, but I did give him brownie points for the getting away from the office bit.

However, the office followed him, and when his phone went off for the third time since we had sat down for dinner, I let out a sigh as he pulled it from his pocket and read the screen. His fingers rapidly moved across the keys.

"Sorry. Again," he said with a tight-lipped smile. "You were saying?"

"I was saying that the gender ultrasound is two weeks from today. I scheduled it for five on Friday afternoon."

He nodded, his mind clearly wandering again. It had been happening a lot lately, even coming through during our daily phone calls.

"What is it?"

He shook his head and tried to plaster on a smile, but it just wasn't reaching his eyes. Something was bothering him and no matter what I tried, I couldn't get it out of him, which only ignited my own fears and reservations.

Was he questioning us? Me? The baby?

It had been growing for weeks, but it took a huge leap the previous weekend. He'd made it obvious work was more important than me, and no amount of tacos and ice cream or hot chocolate were going to make up for it, no matter how good they were.

"I was looking at some places today," I said, trying to break through some of the awkward tension that filled the room, though I had begun to wonder why I was trying so hard.

"Places?"

"Yeah, that neighborhood Jenna and I were looking at. They've had a couple new condos completed."

He made a small humming sound and nodded. It was aggravating. He didn't engage in the conversation, and if he couldn't engage in conversation about where I was going to live, how could I talk to him about the baby? About the other issues going on?

I was supposed to be watching for things that made my blood

pressure spike, and the biggest issue was sitting across the table from me.

He was showing little interest in me or my life, and that was why I hadn't told him about my blood pressure issues or the baby moving. He seemed to have lost interest.

Our kisses lacked the spark they'd once had. My stomach knotted and I tried not to think about why it was missing, but the worry persisted. The separation I felt was on multiple levels, like a disconnect at the core. It left me unsettled and unsure of what to do with those feelings.

There was a pit in my stomach and a fissure formed in my heart.

"I need you to tell me something," I said as we lay in bed that night.

"What?"

"Am I someone you have feelings for, or am I just an obligation?"

His eyes widened, and he reached out to cup my face. "You're not an obligation. I…I care a great deal for you."

"What does that even mean?"

His brow furrowed. "You mean a lot to me, Natasha. So much."

None of the words did anything to assuage the despair that had taken up residence in my chest. There were no declarations of love, just a vague assurance of caring.

I meant a lot to him. He cared for me. Those were things you said to a friend or someone you liked, not someone you'd been in a steady relationship with for over three months and were having a child with.

I nodded and bit down on my lower lip in an attempt to keep the tears at bay. He wrapped his arm around me and in minutes, he was asleep.

I laid awake, tears silently slipping down to the pillowcase. I could feel the heat coming from his body. Though with me physically, he was no longer with me mentally. His priorities had changed somehow, and work was once again the ruler, while I was the afterthought.

The mistress.

The first month or two we were together was nothing but pure happiness and I thought I'd found my soul mate, but the last month I'd begun to seriously question if he'd even be around when the baby came.

And the pain in my chest only served to remind me that I was utterly in love with a man who couldn't put me first in his life.

Chapter
TWENTY

June 5th

Two weeks. That was how long it had been since I'd seen Richard. Two horribly long and gut-wrenching weeks.

Two weeks of thinking about where I stood. I had my answer, but I didn't want to admit it. We were in two different places, literally, and he was never going to let work go.

I stared at the clock on the wall of the doctor's office watching as the seconds ticked by. They turned into minutes, and still no Richard.

He promised.

He promised me that he would be here. This, of all appointments, this was the one for him to make an effort to attend, to show me that he was in this with me. With each second that ticked by, the more I realized that he wasn't coming.

I'd barely heard from him in days, and it had been two weeks since I'd seen him, as work had kept him busy the prior weekend.

After a few minutes, my phone buzzed. My stomach sank, and I knew my fears were true without even looking. Tears filled my eyes, and I blinked them away just in time to hear the door handle turn and see the doctor walk in. It felt like I was on autopilot driving to one of the most important appointments, and I felt off. We went through all the usual checking-in stuff. How were things, had I had any more dizziness, blah, blah, blah.

I'd totally lost my focus due to his absence.

"This is serious, Natasha," Dr. Danvers said. "Every time you've come in, your blood pressure has been elevated, and I'm concerned about hypertension. I'd like to run some blood work, to check your kidney and liver processing. While I don't want to put the Gestational Hypertension—also known as Preeclampsia—label on you, I may be forced to. It's become critical for you to watch your stress levels."

And there it was. Richard was so one foot out the door I couldn't even tell him about my health issues. He didn't seem to care about anything but work lately.

"I don't know what to do."

Her lips formed a thin line. "I think you know what your biggest stressor is, because it's the one thing that is missing from this room right now. The one thing that is missing every time I see you."

I swiped at the tears filling my eyes and nodded, my doctor confirming every negative thought I'd had for weeks.

Richard's distance was the problem. Not the physical separation of our long-distance relationship, but the void that had been deepening between us for over a month.

For my health, I needed to make a choice.

In my mind I begged and pleaded for Richard to walk through that door, to be there for me and the baby, but the moment had come, and he wasn't there.

I stared at the screen, watching the ultrasound tech manipulate around, trying to get a good shot, but our baby was being shy. That or it sensed my distress, hoping that Daddy might arrive just in time to find out if we were having the girl that Richard kept saying he was certain of, or if we were having a boy, which I always said just to be obstinate and tease him.

The culmination of over twenty-three weeks of waiting and wondering, of teasing each other incessantly, and I was alone.

The happiness of the moment was tarnished and grey due to his absence. The baby was fine. I had a printout showing the gender and when I left to check out at the reception desk, there was still no Richard.

And I knew at that moment it was time to make a decision I was not prepared to make. One that broke my heart into a million pieces.

I pulled out my phone and sighed as I unlocked it.

I am so sorry. I just got out of a meeting—Richard

I called Jenna the moment I got in the car, needing to try anything to keep the sobs at bay.

"Hey, babe!" she said excitedly. "So, is it a girl or is it a boy?"

"He wasn't there," I said.

The silence stretched on longer than normal for Jenna, then there was a hissed, "Son of a bitch."

"I can't count on him. I can't count on him to come here." The sobs let loose. All the weeks of holding my feelings at bay, of believing whatever it was that drew Richard and I together initially would be strong enough to see us through the widening chasm, finally overpowered me and I broke. I had trouble getting the words out, my sobs so fierce I could barely understand myself, so it was anyone's guess if Jenna could understand my blubbering speech.

"I can't do this. He doesn't love me. It doesn't matter what I feel for him, because this, us…just isn't gonna work. I'm not important enough to him, and I will always be hurt by his lack of attention. We will both pay if I stay, because I will always be the mistress to his marriage."

There was no holding back the feelings of inadequacy or my tears any longer. They came gushing out, flooding my eyes and streaming down my face.

"I love him, Jenna, but he doesn't love me."

Chapter
TWENTY-ONE

Richard

I took a deep breath. "Fuck, what a week." Every day I'd been in endless meetings.

Despite being the VP, I had been burning the midnight oil with Michael every night. It was easier to sleep on my couch than to go home. Thankfully I kept a change of clothes and a bag of toiletries in my office.

The week had been hell, somehow worse than the prior fiscal year ends. I rubbed at my forehead as I finished up an email, my mind focused on the task.

The phone rang four times, almost switching to voicemail when I got to it. Seeing Natasha's name reminded me what day it was.

Shit!

I'd texted her nearly an hour ago and I still wasn't out.

"I'm on my way," I said as I began logging off my computer.

"Don't bother."

I paused, trying to figure out if I'd heard her correctly. "What?"

"Do you remember what today was?"

"A doctor's appointment. And I'm so sorry. I promise I won't miss the next one," I said, cursing myself out.

"You promised you wouldn't miss *this* one. *This* was the one you needed to be at. I needed you beside me today, and you weren't there."

The hurt in her voice was palpable, and my stomach dropped. "You think I didn't want to be?"

"If you did, wouldn't you have made every effort?" she hissed.

"Fuck, Nat, we live almost two hundred miles apart. I'm the fucking VP of Finance and, as you are *well* aware, we are at the fiscal year end."

She knew that June was always a shit month.

"It's been weeks since I've seen you and days since I got a call."

"I'm busy!" I blew out a breath to calm down. "Come July first things will calm down, but until then, it's seventy-plus-hour work weeks."

There was a knock on my door and my assistant popped his head in, but I waved him away.

"I'm working almost as much, but I guess I'm the only one invested enough to miss you and want to talk to you."

"Don't pull that shit. If you're pissed off, just say it."

"I'm fucking pissed off!" she screamed.

"So am I!" I yelled back. "Did it ever occur to you that my world doesn't revolve around you?"

She drew in a sharp breath, and I internally cursed at myself. "I'm sorr—"

"I don't have to be your world, just your heart, but I'm beginning to think that's never going to happen."

Fuck. I ran my hand down my face, my jaw ticking in aggravation. I hated the way her voice wavered. Hated that I was the reason.

Feelings were hard for me. Difficult to crippling levels, and even harder to express in words.

Being two hundred miles away, words were all I had at that moment, and there were none.

"Nothing?"

"It's not that simple, Natasha."

"Why not?"

"Give me three weeks to get past this shit, and we'll go away for the weekend."

Silence. Fuck.

Silence was not a good sign.

Then, after a heavy breath, Natasha continued, and the defeat was apparent in her voice. "Don't bother. You told me that night you were married to your job, and I was just foolish enough to believe that I could be the one to change that."

The line went silent before I could respond.

Shit.

Fuck!

It took everything in me not to throw the phone at the wall. She didn't even say goodbye, she just hung up. What the hell was I supposed to do with that?

What the hell was I supposed to do with all of it? Didn't she understand how much I was carrying around on my shoulders?

Chapter
TWENTY-TWO

Natasha

It had been two days since I hung up on Richard, and I had yet to leave my bed. I was so upset I blocked his number. Dr. Danvers said to watch my stress, and it was stressing me out more. He was the father of my child, but I needed space.

I regretted doing it almost immediately, but I needed to be strong. If he wanted to fix things, he would come to me.

When I heard voices coming down the hall, I started, but relaxed back into my blanket fort when I recognized my mother.

"You know," I whined from under the covers. "I didn't give you that key so you could just walk in whenever."

"All right, young lady, get up," Mom said from the doorway to my bedroom.

"No," I whined from under the covers. I didn't want to do anything but wallow in my misery…and pizza. And ice cream, pickles, fried rice, and bacon cheeseburgers.

My stomach rumbled at all the food thoughts, the baby demanding everything.

Just like when I was a teenager, my mom pulled the covers from me. I cracked an eye and glared at her.

"Don't give me that attitude."

A figure appeared behind my mom, her baby belly entering

first. "I have a milkshake," Hannah said with a smile as she wiggled the Styrofoam cup in front of her. "It's chocolate." Her voice was sing-song and way too cheerful right now, but she had a milkshake.

My other eye opened, and I lifted my head from the pillow. Damn her.

With each step, her brunette waves gave a slight bounce, her blue eyes sparkling. She was trying to cheer me up, and she had me at "milkshake."

I took a long pull, which was how long it took to get the ultra-thick shake up the straw. When the cold hit my tongue, it burst into multiple layers of chocolate heaven and I let out a moan, my body sagging.

"Told you." Hannah looked back to my mom.

"What are you two doing here?" I asked before attempting to pull more up the straw.

"Jenna called," Mom said. There was a sad smile on her face, and I swallowed hard before looking away.

"He'll come around," Hannah assured.

"If he hasn't by now, he's not going to." My heart gave way to another crack. "I thought he was everything, that I meant something, and maybe I do, but not more than work." I took another long pull. "I want *Portillo's*."

"Get yourself dressed and we will go," Mom said. The cheerful edge to her voice did not inspire me like it did her dog.

I shook my head. "I'll have it delivered."

"No, you're coming with us," Hannah said. "We're going to go shopping. You don't have anything for the baby yet."

It wasn't entirely true. In the corner of my room sat a basket, one that held a few items Richard and I had bought together, including the onesie and the teddy bear.

A tear fell from my eye and slid down my cheek. Hannah's thumb swiped it away, and she tapped my chin to make me turn toward her.

"It's a shit situation."

"How would you know?" I asked her.

Hannah and I had been talking a lot more than we had before due to the babies, but she had my brother, who was devoted to her and had been for years.

It was a bitch thing to say, but I wasn't in the mood to be reasoned with. I just wanted to stay bundled up in my comforter.

"It hasn't always been wine and roses with your brother, you know. This isn't the end. It's not really over. This is a hiccup."

"It's one hell of a hiccup."

She pushed a lock of hair behind my ear. "Some are worse than others, no lie, but have faith that Richard will be back."

"Do I even want him back?" It was a solid question, one I wasn't even sure I knew the answer to.

"I can't answer that, but from the state of you right now, I'd say yes. Look, I don't know what happened between you two, but it's obvious you have deep feelings for him. So, get up, brush your hair, and get your ass dressed, and let's go get something to eat, then waddle around the baby store and pick out cribs."

I took another long pull of shake. "I don't waddle."

"Maybe not yet, but you will. We both will."

They gave me twenty minutes to make myself presentable, and what I managed was base-line. I couldn't remember the last time I gave so few fucks about how I looked. Yoga pants, tennis shoes, a T-shirt that stretched around my stomach, and a duster sweater that hit my knees.

I ordered the works at *Portillo's*—Italian beef sandwich (wet with peppers), cheese fries, and a chocolate cake shake.

And I cried when I ate every last bite.

They dragged me to the baby store, and I stared dispassionately at the furniture displays. Twenty-four weeks along, and I had nothing for my baby. No room, no basic necessities, and no father. Time was running out, and I was so ill prepared. I'd been too busy playing house and not seeing that I would always be second best.

Work was important, but there needed to be balance, and Richard dug his heels in, refusing to even entertain balance. If work contacted him, it took priority over everything.

"What do you think of this crib, Nat?" Hannah asked, drawing me over.

"It's nice," I said, taking in the white color and the rest of the collection. It really was a nice set with a matching dresser and rocking chair. I sat down in the chair, loving the way it swiveled as well as rocked, and smoothed my hands over my stomach.

For forty-eight nerve-wracking hours, I had pondered what I was going to do with a baby by myself when I first found out. Then Richard appeared and it was no longer just me, it was "we." In the months that followed it was the two of us, envisioning life with our child.

But sometimes fantasies are just that, and sometimes reality is not as reliable or steady as you thought.

"I need a bigger place," I said, gaining Hannah's attention. "Can Carson help me move?"

She gave me a sad smile. "Of course. Are you looking at places?"

I nodded. "I've had my eye on this condo community by the river. Want to go see it?"

"Sure."

I wasn't going to count on Richard to be there, not anymore. I had to move forward, to plan for life with a baby and joint custody.

To plan for a life without Richard beside me.

Part of that meant keeping my job and staying off bed rest.

Chapter TWENTY-THREE

Richard

Work kept me busy over the weekend and all of Monday, but even having all my focus on work could not stop the weight from settling on my chest or the pit that grew in my stomach every day. They weren't feelings I was familiar with, but I knew they had to do with Natasha.

Calling and texting had been futile exercises—she wasn't answering.

We were both angry, and the distance didn't help.

Though I wasn't sure if it was her I was angry with. It was me. After she hung up on me, I realized why she was so upset. I'd missed a pivotal moment I could never get back in the life of my child. A moment when I should have been holding her hand and kissing her in excitement, and instead I was sitting at a conference table, firmly planting another wall between us.

Why I kept doing it, I had no idea. My self-destructive moves were hurting more than just me. The walls were meant to protect me, but they were doing the opposite.

I wanted to let her in. I wanted to drown in the feelings that washed over me when we were together. To forever be the man I had been the night I met her. A man whose entire being was focused solely on her.

But in Chicago was every reminder of Desiree and her betrayal. It wasn't the home we shared, but the city that was infected with years of memories.

The only time I'd ever opened my heart, I fell head over heels in love. I was devoted to Desiree to a fault, and I failed to see the signs until I caught them together.

It destroyed me, destroyed my ability to trust anyone. And until Natasha hung up on me, I hadn't realized how that included her.

I hadn't meant to distrust her. She gave me no reason to, but it was ingrained in those walls. It wasn't love I was keeping out, it was trust.

But Natasha wasn't Desiree, and the emotions that bound me were deeper than I'd ever experienced. So much deeper than the love I once had for Desiree.

The terror that had paralyzed me for days was…

My phone went off with Natasha's ringtone, and I scrambled to reach it across the expanse of my cluttered desk.

Her name flashed across my screen, and I blew out a breath in a sort of relief. She hadn't replied to my texts or called back since our fight.

"Hi," I said, frozen in anticipation.

"Richard, it's Jenna."

My brow scrunched in confusion before a spike of fear struck my chest. "What's wrong?"

"Nat fainted about an hour ago. She hit her head pretty hard. They just left to take her to the hospital."

Time stopped.

"What hospital?" I managed to choke out.

"What are you going to do?" she asked.

"I'm fucking coming. What hospital?"

I was out of my chair and running toward the elevator in seconds, ignoring Michael as he called my name.

Nothing was going to stop me from getting to her.

The hours it took me to get there felt like an eternity.

I swallowed hard. My stomach rolled, and an enormous pressure settled in my chest. The closer I got to her, the more utter despair crashed down on me.

When I entered her room, I almost couldn't breathe. It may have only been a fall, but what if it had been worse? What if something bad had happened and I wasn't with her?

Monitors pinged, and there was some kind of strap around her stomach. Gauze circled her head, her right eye swollen.

"Natasha?" I whispered, reaching out to stroke her cheek, but there was no response.

"Oh, you're here," Jenna said from the door, a bottle and some snack bags in her hand.

"Is she okay?" I asked as I sat in the chair next to the bed.

"She hit her head, but it's just some bruising and swelling. She woke up for a minute, but fell right back asleep."

"How? Why?"

"They told her mom it was a combination of things. Stress with your breakup—"

"We didn't break up," I interrupted. We had a fight, that was all. Right?

"That's not what she thinks. I had to unblock your number from her phone."

It felt like I'd been doused in ice. That was why she hadn't responded. Had I hurt her that badly? Had my actions forced her to cut me from her life?

"Anyway, added in the stress from work, the pregnancy, and her high blood pressure. She's been miserable, and it all came to a head."

"Miserable?" The word caught in my throat.

Miserable. I had made the mother of my child miserable. It was all my fault because I'd fucked up.

I finally saw it.

All the ways I'd pushed her away, created a distance between the two of us. The walls weren't enough, I had created an abyss of space over weeks.

The one person I wanted to make happy, to take care of, and I'd managed to do the exact opposite.

"All you have to do is tell her how you feel."

I shook my head. "She's too perfect for me."

Jenna quirked a brow at me. "Nat is far from perfect."

"To me she is." I stroked her hand with my thumb.

"Then why can't you tell her that? Why can't you tell her how you feel about her?"

I jumped up from my seat and began pacing. "It's not that simple." That pain in my chest ignited, and I couldn't sit still.

"Yes, it actually is. Either you love her or you don't."

"Maybe that's how you operate, Jenna, but that's not how I do."

Her eyes narrowed on me. "I can tell, and so can she. All she wants is the man you were the night you met."

"I don't know who I was that night. I was in some sort of trance, completely drowning in her, needing to be close to her. Wanting her in ways I've never wanted anyone else."

I wanted that night to never end.

"Once again, what is the problem?"

"The problem is me," I growled. "The problem is that I am afraid that if I admit how I feel, she'll have the power to destroy me."

Her eyebrows shot up. "I hate to be the bearer of bad news, but you gave her that power already."

"What do you mean?" I asked.

"This second, you aren't her boyfriend, just her asshole boss, and that knowledge causes you pain. You gave her the power to destroy you, and by not admitting to her how you feel, *you* activated it."

I stared at her before stepping back over to my chair and sitting back down. Was she right? Was my inability to tell her, my drive to protect myself, the catalyst for my own self-destruction that tore down the best thing in my life?

"I don't know how to change. I think about her constantly when I'm away. There's this thrumming in my veins when we're apart that drives me mad, but once I see her, touch her." I took her hand in mine again. "It's like the world is right again."

"Do you love her?" Jenna asked.

"I don't know," I said, though I knew it wasn't right.

"Yes, you do. So here's my advice—get your fucking head screwed back on right, or you will lose her forever. Do you want that?"

I shook my head. What I wanted was to be closer to her, not farther away. I wanted to be rid of the pain and doubt that clouded my judgment. That thought walls were the answer. They weren't. The only thing they did was keep me alone, and I didn't want that anymore.

My phone went off again, buzzing with another message. For hours I'd ignored it, ignored the calls and texts. I told my assistant to handle shit, and it seemed he wasn't handling it.

"I'll let you stew on that," Jenna said as she stood. "I'll be back."

I drew Natasha's hand to my lips. "I'm sorry. I've fucked up. Badly."

There was only one way to make it right, Jenna was correct there, but I wasn't sure I could do it yet. To face those emotions was terrifying.

A few minutes after Jenna disappeared, the door opened and a doctor not much older than me walked in.

"Hello, I'm Dr. Nadar," he said with a smile before walking over to the computer.

"Is the baby okay?" I asked, desperate to know.

"And you are?"

"The father."

He nodded, apparently deeming me a viable person to speak with. "The baby is fine, and we're monitoring her."

"Her?"

The doctor blinked at me, then scanned her chart. "It looks like she had a gender ultrasound last week."

"Yes. I...I missed it." For something that was completely unimportant, but told myself it was more important than that ultrasound. A moment I didn't get to share with her.

"When can I take her home?" I asked.

"We're going to keep her tonight to monitor her condition. Her numbers are still elevated."

Still elevated? "Which numbers?"

"Her blood pressure is the biggest issue. Hypertension is a serious condition and can cause everything from swelling to liver failure."

Hypertension? Liver failure? When did her blood pressure become an issue?

"When did that start?"

He scrolled through her chart. "Looks like it started showing up around the beginning of her second trimester. Quite a bit earlier than we usually see, which was cause for concern."

The information hit me hard. She'd kept things from me. Aspects that I needed to be aware of. Why didn't she tell me her blood pressure had become a problem? Whenever I noticed something was wrong, she brushed it off as just another pregnancy symptom.

Then a thought shot through me with a force like being hit by a truck. The date. The weekend that I realized my feelings for her were stronger than I could allow. The weekend I threw the first walls up between us. The offhand comment Natasha had made about her second trimester starting.

I'd pushed her away, so far, in fact, she felt she couldn't confide in me. As I built walls around me, I tore down the chains that connected us.

She'd been quieter, withdrawn almost, when we were together. I was working more and saw her less, and when I did she was reserved. In recent weeks, the passion that once burned so hot was barely a glow, and I'd chalked it up to no longer being in the honeymoon phase.

That wasn't it at all.

It was me.

I recounted everything. The meme war she'd started had failed to pick back up one Monday. Over the last two months our calls and text messaging dwindled, and lately it wasn't uncommon for us to go days in between contact. Again, it wasn't her…it was me. I was the one who stopped responding.

I'd put everything before her and pushed her to the background. Why? Because there, maybe she wouldn't have as strong of an effect on me? That I could somehow manage my feelings for her if she wasn't my sole focus?

That proved to be a useless exercise.

"Richard?"

I looked up to find Natasha's mom and dad standing in the doorway.

The air was suddenly thick with tension. I didn't know how much they knew, but given how close they were, I was certain they knew everything. And none of it painted me in a very good light. Which only made me their least favorite person at that moment.

"Do you really think you should be here?" Greg asked.

I deserved the hit, but that didn't make the blow any easier to take.

"She needs me."

"She's needed you for a lot longer than today, and where have you been?" He drilled in further.

At least I finally knew where Natasha got it from. Her father was every bit as direct as she was.

"Not where I should have been," I answered honestly.

"It's a good thing Wyatt and Carson don't know you're here. Just saying," he said, his expression tight.

I clenched my jaw and kept silent. Knowing he had every right to his statements didn't make them any easier to hear.

Tabitha put her hand on her husband's arm, gaining his attention. "Come on."

"Come on where? I came to see my daughter."

"And you've seen her. Now, let's give them some space."

Greg leaned down and pressed his lips to Natasha's forehead. "Love you, Natty." His eyes caught mine as he straightened, and I didn't miss the warning there.

The interaction hit me in a way I wasn't expecting. Greg was a man simply protecting his only daughter. Would I react any other way if our positions were switched? If it was our daughter lying on the bed, knowing the man beside her was the cause of so much of her pain?

Shortly after they left, Natasha's hand twitched in mine and she let out a low groan. Her eyes flitted open, and she turned to me.

"Hi," I said when her beautiful eyes met mine. My chest clenched as the look in her eyes deadened.

"What are you doing here, Richard?" she asked. The strength was gone from her voice. Had I really reduced her to such a shadow of herself?

"You're hurt."

Her eyes narrowed on me, though the action caused the swollen one to shut. "You actually left work, drove all the way down here, because I fainted?"

"Yes," I answered.

"It's year end," she ground out.

"Yes."

She eyed me for a moment. "You actually left?"

I took her hand in mine and drew it to my lips. My other hand drew lazy circles across the bump that held our baby. Trusting those feelings was difficult, but I forced down the walls that had started to build up between us. Being honest with her and myself was the only way we were going to make it through. "Why didn't you tell me?"

Her brow scrunched. "Tell you what?"

"That we're having a girl."

"Because I figured if you couldn't be bothered to come to an appointment that was on your schedule for almost a month, you didn't care."

I squeezed her hand. "I do care, Nat."

"Even so, you still didn't care enough to come," she snapped.

"Don't."

She pulled her hand from mine. "Don't lash out in anger and frustration? Don't show you how I feel?" She shook her head, her eyes narrowed on me. "I'm sorry, Richard, but not telling people emotions is your hang-up, not mine."

"You're not wrong."

With that, Natasha's eyes closed and her head turned slowly away, shutting me out. Forcing me to look back at the last few weeks without the blinders I'd been wearing. All they did was make me lose focus on the things I cared about, instead of keeping out those that could hurt me.

Chapter
TWENTY-FOUR

Natasha

When I was released the next morning, it was Richard who was there to drive me home.

I hated it. I hated the way it made my chest clench to see him there, so attentive to my needs. It was a side of him I'd seen glimpses of in the past, but it had been many weeks since this side of him had been allowed out.

The buzzing of his phone in his pocket went unnoticed, and the ringing through the car's speakers went unanswered.

"You aren't going to get that? It could be important." The air continued to be filled with static, and it was suffocating.

He reached across the center console and covered my hand with his, giving it a squeeze. "Not as important as you."

"Had some epiphany, huh?" I cringed against the light, my eyes overly sensitive thanks to the migraine slamming my head into a table had caused.

"I want to talk about this."

"Why?" *Give me a reason.*

"Because this isn't over, despite what you seem to think. One fight does not end a relationship."

"It is over, and if you think a fight is why we broke up, you really have no idea what the fuck is going on."

"I've been flaky, I know."

I scoffed at that and pulled my hand from his, crossing my arms over my chest. "That's one way to describe the last month. Hell, the last two months."

"Do you have a more accurate term?"

"Checked out? Running for the door? Leaving without saying goodbye?" My voice broke on the last few words, and I clenched my jaw to hold back tears. For weeks I'd wanted an open and honest conversation with him, but he continued to slip further and further away instead. "Actions speak loudly, Richard, and you are a dichotomy of actions. On one side, you are affectionate and sexy and caring and everything I've ever hoped to find in a man. On the other side, you completely disregard everything that isn't work, and that includes me."

"I'm in a high-level position that requires a lot of time."

"But not *all* of your time," I said, hoping maybe he would understand. "You're allowed to have a personal life, to have a life outside of the office, but you refuse to set any type of boundaries. You're available to them twenty-four seven."

He remained silent for the last mile, hopefully mulling over my words in a constructive way, otherwise the rest of this conversation was going to go sideways. When he pulled into a spot in front of my door, he had me wait so he could help me out of the car. He even made me hang on to his arm as we walked inside in case I got dizzy.

After helping me out of my work clothes and into something comfortable, he helped me to the couch. I didn't really need the help, but he was insistent. The swelling in my right eye persisted, causing limited vision out of that eye, so I allowed it.

However, that meant he remained in my presence. He scooted the sofa chair around so that he was sitting in front of me. It seemed we were about to have a conversation I didn't want. I said my piece. Now I wanted to move on. Before I could ask him to leave, Richard noticed the boxes stacked around the room.

Carson had delivered a bunch of moving boxes and the flattened ones were leaning against the wall. On the kitchen table sat two boxes that were taped up. There were more on the floor stacked up. The walls were bare, and so were the shelves of my entertainment center. Slowly my life was being packed up.

"What the hell is going on?" he asked, and I was surprised by the anger lacing his tone.

I shrugged my shoulders. "I'm moving to a bigger place next month."

"Without talking to me?"

With a nonchalance that I didn't feel, I calmly responded. "I have a baby coming in eighteen weeks. I can't wait for you to make decisions any longer. It's time for action."

"Okay. We didn't discuss this." His voice was strained and he blew out a breath. I held back my urge to scream at him that I'd tried to talk to him about it and he ignored me. "Move in with me. Come to Chicago."

My eyes widened, and I stared at him. "What?"

His jaw was set. "You can stay with the company, just in a different department."

I blinked and shook my head. "If this is your version of a grand gesture, you'd better think of something better." He was only saying it because he felt guilty.

His eyes were wide in disbelief that I wasn't suddenly swooning over his declaration. How could I? I didn't want him to want to be with me out of guilt or obligation.

"Natasha."

I held up my hand. "What you've just said is that you want me to leave Indianapolis and move to Chicago. Leave my family and friends and job to live with you. Is that correct?"

"Yes."

I pursed my lips and shook my head. "No. Fuck, no."

"Why not?"

"Because my life is here. You're asking me to leave my life, pack it up, leave my support system with a baby on the way for a place where I don't have that support, and really neither do you. Yes, you make more money, but we work for the same company."

"Which creates other issues, because I'm technically your boss."

"Four steps removed."

"That doesn't change the reality. My position makes me the boss of every employee below me, even if they don't report to me. But you do report to me. You are in my direct department."

Tears began to fill my eyes. "Once again, your job comes before me."

"Nat, that's not—"

"That's not the reason? I love you, Richard."

He stared at me in stunned silence but made no move to speak, which made the tears flow down my cheeks.

"I've been in love with you for so long, ever since we met, but I see now that you will never love me. And even if you do, you will never love me with the depth that I love you. I don't know why, but I do know all that awaits me with you is heartache and pain."

"I…I have difficulty expressing my feelings in words."

I was getting tired of his excuses, and I'd had enough. "Your actions have spoken loud enough. We'll go through the court system to set up custody and a schedule."

"No," he ground out.

"It's the easiest way."

He shook his head. "You're asking me to miss half my child's life, Natasha."

"Work will do that regardless. Maybe this will force you to take weekends off."

His eyes were wide, pleading. "Don't do this."

"You're the one doing this, Richard. All I'm doing is protecting myself."

"Please, Nat, don't. Don't leave me."

Don't leave him? "You were never really with me to begin with.

I was just an afterthought, something to do in the few hours outside of your marriage. I'm the other woman, Richard, and I deserve better than that."

He shook his head. "I'm not giving us up. I won't. I refuse to."

I angled my head toward the door. "You should go."

He took my hand in his. "Please, Nat. Don't."

A tear slipped down my cheek. "I have to. For me, for my heart, for our baby, I have to be selfish, no matter how much it hurts, because if I don't stand with my convictions, you'll continue on and the hurt will be so much worse."

The broken expression he wore tore at me. "I won't. I can change. I will change. I just need you to give me a chance to."

I slowly pulled my hand from him. "I need more than empty words and reassurances. I need proof."

"Me being here isn't proof enough?" he asked as he brushed back a lock of hair from my face.

I shook my head. "I'm sorry, but no. It's too little, too late."

He shook his head. "No, not too late. I'm not fucking giving up on this, on us, and I'm going to prove it to you."

He took my face in his hands and I stiffened, then melted when his lips pressed against mine. That connection, that feeling of perfection together lit up, then died down when he released me. He stroked my cheek, his breathing hard, brows scrunched.

"Don't shut me out. Answer my texts. I'm coming for you."

Chapter
TWENTY-FIVE

Richard

I wasn't entirely sure how I got home. The whole drive back to Chicago I felt numb. My brain didn't get on board until the next day when I sat at my desk with my view of Lake Michigan. The sun streamed in, and the beach was studded with bodies enjoying the warm weather. They were seemingly carefree, having a day off with no worries.

There was nothing but turmoil inside me.

I'd lost her.

Each minute away from Natasha burned in ways I'd never experienced before. Weighted down with responsibilities, I'd been choosing the wrong ones to focus on.

It hadn't been twenty-four hours since I left her, but I'd never had a black cloud of this magnitude take up residence in my chest. Not even after my divorce, after finding out Desiree had been cheating on me, did I feel the depth of despair that weighed me down now.

I was determined to make good on my promise, but my normal problem-solving mind had left for vacation and was unavailable to help me figure out what to do.

There was a knock on my door, and I didn't even have a chance to say anything before Michael stepped in.

"Richard, what the hell is going on? You disappeared for days and now you're sitting here, staring out the window." Michael was the president, and was right to be concerned about my recent behavior.

"My girlfriend was taken to the hospital."

Michael blinked at me, his eyes wide. "Girlfriend?"

The fact that only my assistant even knew about Natasha was a telltale sign of my many mistakes.

"She fainted, but she and the baby are okay."

"Baby?" The surprise and shock on his face were noticeable.

I looked up at him. "I need to make some changes."

"Why didn't you tell me you had a girlfriend?" he asked. "Let alone a baby on the way."

That was the million-dollar question.

"I don't know. I went on. Business as usual, counting down the days of the week until I could see her again." I shook my head, not believing the mess I'd made. "They were stolen moments in time heading toward an expiration date."

"What are you talking about?" he asked.

"Any relationship with me is just a ticking time bomb, but I thought maybe if I could just keep it together until the baby was born, maybe she wouldn't see my faults. That was stupid. Natasha sees me as nobody else ever has or ever will. Now I've fucked it all up. She got hurt, and when I tried to show her I was there, show her I care, that I wanted her in my life and to take care of her, she called me out again."

There was no hiding from her, but somehow all my insecurities and doubts disappeared when I was with her. I wanted her in my life. I couldn't imagine not waking up every day with her and our daughter.

"I need to move to Indianapolis."

One of Michael's eyebrows shot up. I'd simply spit the words, but as soon as they were out, I knew they were the right ones. The ones that would get me closer to Natasha.

"Can the VP position be moved?" I asked.

He shook his head. "It can't. I'm sorry, it's just not a possibility. I need you here."

Well, that just made my decision easier.

Chapter TWENTY-SIX

Natasha

After my fall and subsequent hospital stay, I was directed to take the rest of the week off. It was torture the first day after Richard left. There was nothing to do but wallow in my grief. No matter what declarations he made or the love I had for him, I had to let him go.

That knowledge, that it was for the well-being of me and our baby, didn't make it any easier. The acknowledgment that he was the biggest stressor in my life and that stress was causing physical problems with my pregnancy was the hardest truth I'd ever had to face.

What ifs floated through my mind. Would his avoidance have been the same if I'd lived in Chicago? Would he have gone to appointments, or would work have sucked him in all the same?

Jenna came over that night and held me as I sobbed. Just her being there meant the world to me.

She also unblocked his number from my phone.

On Wednesday I felt steady enough to get up, to get my mind something to think about other than Richard. I continued on with the packing, making sure to not overdo it and go slow. For five years I'd lived in the same one-bedroom apartment. It was my first home, and it would be hard to leave it.

I wouldn't miss my neighbors, though. Except Jenna. Her lease was up in September, and her plan was still to buy a condo in the same neighborhood. However, I had a feeling when she moved it would be into Brent's house.

I was so happy for her, but at that moment, I was also a little jealous. Why did I have to fall for a man who was so emotionally stunted?

That wasn't even it. He freely gave affection and showed he cared in so many ways, but when it came to the deeper ones, he couldn't.

I miss you—Richard, came in that afternoon when I was boxing up all the clothes I couldn't fit into anymore.

I stared down at it, my chest clenching. Did I respond? Or ignore? He asked me to reply to his texts, but it was a statement. Yes, I wanted to tell him I missed him, too, but the flip in my stomach reminded me why I shouldn't. If I gave in, nothing would change.

By Friday I'd used all the boxes Carson brought over. It was a little premature, seeing as I hadn't even completed the purchase, but at least I was mostly ready.

Twenty-three weeks down...

I got sucked into binging an Annex original love story after gorging myself on chips and salsa. It was a stupid move, because I was sobbing halfway through.

"Love sucks," I said with a groan as I tossed another tissue into the wastebasket. The baby flipped in my stomach, and I ran my hand across my ever-growing bump. "I'm sorry, baby." My bottom lip quivered and tears filled my eyes, my hand never stopping its path up and down.

For a brief moment after waking to find Richard beside me I had hope that things would change, but it was fleeting. He was untrustworthy with my heart, but I had given it to him with ease. I fell hard and fast, and the brakes were out.

I hadn't heard from him since the text telling me he missed me. For all his declarations, I was certain work had sucked him right back in.

It was after five when my doorbell went off, which confused me. Jenna usually walked right in.

I swung the door open and stared up at the hulk of a man standing in my doorway, my jaw slack.

"Natasha?" he asked in a deep, reverberating tone.

"Me?" I shook my head. "I mean, yes?" I was confused as to who he was and why he was at my door.

"Hey, Nat," Keenan said with a wave from behind the broad shoulders blocking my doorway.

The stranger stepped back, exposing Keenan as he stepped closer. My stomach flipped at the sight of him. If he was standing in front of me, Richard had to be close.

I wrapped my cardigan around me as my brow furrowed. "What's going on?"

"I really need you to come with me."

"Why? Is everything okay?" The atmosphere didn't project fear or worry, so I was confused as to why Keenan was at my door.

"Will you trust me?" he asked as he held out his hand.

While Keenan had never given me any reason not to trust him, there was also the fact that he was Richard's best friend, and I wasn't so much in the trusting mood with him.

I glanced behind him, at the longer looking Mercedes taking over the two spots next to my car.

My anxiety kicked up. That car would take me to Richard, I knew it would. Did I want to see him? Could I handle it?

I glanced down. Had I showered? Yes. My hair was a mess, I was in yoga pants and a T-shirt that stretched greatly around my stomach, which only served as a reminder that I needed some maternity shirts.

My swollen little piggies were the only thing not covered.

"Let me get some shoes," I said before retreating into my bedroom. It was warm out, so I shed my cardigan and slipped on some flip flops. I couldn't help but give myself a cursory once over in the mirror. I looked terrible, my left eye a colorful array of purples and yellows, but there was nothing that could be done. At least most of the swelling around my eye was gone. It was still a little swollen, but most of the puffiness was in the area surrounding my stitches at my brow bone.

I freshened up my ponytail, grabbed my purse, and headed out. Keenan took my arm, making sure I was steady going down the steps, and the driver held open the door for me to slide in.

The extra length I'd seen was in the back seat, giving plenty of room for even the longest of legs. Plush leather, exquisite stitching, and I could swear it had a leg rest that folded out.

We weren't even out of the neighborhood when he spoke. "I wanted to talk to you."

"Okay."

"I heard what happened with Rick."

I pursed my lips and looked down at my hands. "Why are you here?"

"Because you need to know I've never seen him as happy as he is with you. He's fucked things up, in only the way Rick can."

"What does that mean?"

He blew out a breath. "Rick's divorce fucked him up in ways I don't think he ever understood. Then you came along and turned everything he ever knew upside down. You were it. The girl."

"I thought that, too."

"You are, though." He turned in his seat, his eyes beseeching me. "It was like lightning when you two came together."

His description wasn't wrong. That was what it felt like when we met—lightning.

"With my divorce, I dealt with my feelings. I processed them and came to terms with them, but that was never something he did. Rick shut them off. Buried them like you'd bury a well, and kept them locked up there until the second his eyes met yours."

It made sense, as much as I didn't want to believe it. It happened one day, like a switch was thrown. That was when things began to fall apart.

"What does it matter now? Even if he finally admits he loves me, it doesn't change anything. He's still married to his job, devoted to it and only it, not me." My voice trailed off and I swallowed back a hitch that was threatening to turn into another sob.

He reached out and gave my hand a squeeze. "You woke him up to his stupidity. It's hard to change, to let go of baggage you've carried around for years. He got comfortable, but I can tell you he's way out of that comfort zone now."

"What does that mean?" I asked.

The car slowed down, and I scanned the street. We were in a neighborhood, sitting in front of a large modern colonial. There was a for sale sign in the yard.

My brow scrunched as I looked at the home. "What's this?"

"Just keep an open mind," Keenan said as the driver exited the car.

He held the door open and took my hand, helping me from the car. Keenan came around and took my arm again. I didn't exactly like the coddling feeling, but after my fall, I wasn't going to turn it down.

As we walked up the sidewalk that led to the front door, Richard emerged. He was wearing jeans and a T-shirt, his hands stuffed in his pockets.

I stopped ten feet from him.

Keenan gave him a nod, which Richard returned.

"Thanks, man," Richard said.

"Good luck!" Keenan said before leaning down and giving me a kiss on the cheek, then headed back to the car.

I crossed my arms in front of me to keep myself in place, to keep from running into his arms. I missed him so much, but I wasn't going to just cave. "What is all this?"

Richard tilted his head toward the house. "Come take a look."

"At what?"

"Just come look." He held out his hand, but I ignored it, instead climbing the steps and walking right past him.

I wanted to know what this was all about, and I didn't want to get my hopes up that it was something good. If it meant I had to be cold, I had to be, even though all I wanted was his arms wrapped around me.

My tightly clenched jaw relaxed, my lips parted as I walked into the two-story entry. Hardwood floors flowed seamlessly from one room to the next. To the right was an office, to the left a formal dining room.

Transom windows hung over every entry, and nine-foot ceilings gave it an open feel.

I stepped forward and stopped when I got to the entrance of the kitchen. It was beautiful. Ideal in its décor and finishes. White cabinets with a grey granite counter, large island with beautiful pendant lights, double oven, gas stove, and a walk-in pantry.

There was a kitchen table with lots of room for daily meals. I could envision sitting at it while we helped children with homework.

I shook my head and looked toward the family room. "Oh, come on," I whispered. Another ideal room. The ceilings were coffered, and there was a gas burning fireplace with built-ins on either side. On one wall were two sets of French doors.

I knew he was steps behind me, observing me, but I was transfixed by everything, especially the large screened-in porch I was walking out to. It was the perfect entertaining size, complete with a wood-burning fireplace, and overlooked a large fenced backyard with a swimming pool and a small lake just beyond, lined on the far side with trees.

There was a fully finished walk-out basement with eight-foot ceilings, complete with a wet bar, movie room, home gym, game room, and full bathroom.

As we looked around at the home, the memories of long-ago conversations filtered in.

The master bedroom was the perfect size with a tray ceiling and bay window. There was a large bathroom with a steam shower and jetted tub. The closet was an entire other room and big enough to have a chest of drawers in the center, creating a table with drawers.

There were four more bedrooms, each one grand in size with the same tray ceilings. The smallest one was about the size of my current bedroom.

"What do you think?" Richard asked when we returned to the main floor.

I gobbled up all the sights, filing away the features for my dream home. "It's absolutely beautiful, but I still don't understand why I'm here."

"This could be our home."

My head snapped in his direction, my eyes wide as my heart flipped in my chest. I heard him wrong, I had to have. "What?"

He stepped closer, his eyes on mine as he reached for my hand. "If you love it, this could be our home. It's as close as I can come to giving you your dream home, but I want to share the dream with you."

My dream home?

He had been listening. At a time when the space between us was growing daily, it was an innocuous conversation I didn't think he'd really paid attention to. Standing in a place that *felt* like home, that had all the features on my dream list, I found out he had. To every last detail, he had.

"I've experienced how love can turn on you. How it can break your life apart. By the time I was your age, I'd already had my dreams of a football career decimated, and then was married and divorced."

"These are all things I know."

"What you have to understand is how those things shaped our relationship." His jaw tightened and he stepped closer until there were only a few inches separating us. "The deeper things got, the more I cared about you, the more fear crept in. Subconsciously I began pulling away, putting up walls to protect myself and the life I'd built."

I swallowed and nodded. "And oh, how your life was going to change."

"It's not uncommon. I had this wonderful night with you, and the next time I see you it's 'oh, hey, Richard. Guess what? You're going to be a dad!' and at the time I took it in stride. But my mind betrayed me. It sat back there and though I knew the reality of things. I kept doing what I do best—looking for the logistics. How was it going to work? Where would we live? My condo isn't equipped for a baby."

Once again, his thought process was focused on him. "Not winning any points here."

"In a perfect world, nothing would stop me from being with you. But I'm not perfect. I told you that the first night. Something inside me is broken, and I know you're the only one that can fix it."

Tears filled my eyes and I willed them away. "This better not be your apology, because it doesn't work."

He shook his head and took my other hand in his, bringing them together between his. "No. You were right. I was being selfish and asking too much of you, blaming it on my career. So I changed my path."

I blinked at him, at the smile on his face. Time seemed to stop as I attempted to process the meaning. "You what?"

"Michael told me I couldn't move the position, because we work hand in hand, so I gave it up," he said, his gaze never leaving mine. My heart pounded in my chest as I listened. "As of yesterday, I am no longer an employee of Annex, but am now owner of Bennett Sports Advisors. As of yesterday, my condo is for sale, and as of today I'm looking for a house to raise our family in Indianapolis."

My brow scrunched as tears filled my eyes. I grabbed onto his collar. "That isn't what I wanted, Richard." I just wanted to be loved and respected. I didn't want to completely upend his life. It wasn't my intent for him to leave his job and move to Indianapolis.

He cupped my face, bringing my eyes back to his. "But it's what I want. Being married to my job only caused me to be unhappy. It was all I did, all I thought about, because it was also my escape. An escape I used too much and too often. I want my time to be with you. I want to be married to you."

My heart skipped and the baby did a backflip. "W-what?"

He leaned down, his forehead resting against mine. "I'm in love with you, Natasha. I was just too scared to say it, and that fear led me to wrecking the happiest time of my life. You're the air I breathe, the blood in my veins. I'm yours. Totally and completely."

My gaze flitted between his eyes, and I saw nothing but absolute truth. He was willing to give up everything, to start over, in order to be with me. A clean break from all the memories that dragged him down on a daily basis.

I believed every word. How could I not?

He loved me, and he proved it with actions and not just the words he was finally able to say.

My vision blurred and a sob broke from me as I threw my arms around his shoulders.

"I love you, Richard."

All the walls and space between us melted away with each tear that fell.

He listened. He finally understood. I wanted to find a compromise together, but he gave me the greatest gift he ever could—he gave me himself.

It wasn't a sacrifice, it was a rebirth.

"I love you. So much," he said as he cradled me in his arms. "Do you want to live here? We can look at other houses, I just—"

I pressed my finger to his lips. "I want this house." I wanted the memories of what it represented. It was everything, and I didn't need to see any others.

"You're sure?"

I nodded. "I want to raise our family here."

He pressed his lips to mine. "Me too." He took hold of my hand and led me to the porch. The sound of the crickets chirping filled the air and we sat down on the loveseat. I curled into his side as he pulled out his phone.

I froze, and he felt it, turning the phone toward me. "How much should we offer?"

I balked at the list price. It was a huge house, and I knew it was a great school system. I also knew his condo would sell for hundreds of thousands more.

"Full price."

"All in?"

I nodded. "I don't want to lose it."

It was a good thing I hadn't finished the purchase of the condo, because I was so in love with the walls surrounding us. It wasn't just the fixtures and the layout, it was the thought he put into picking this one. It was perfect, and I knew it would be perfect for us.

"When can we move in?"

"I bet we could request a short closing."

"Good, because my apartment is ready to go."

"I can't wait to be sitting out here, looking out at the lake while we play with our little girl." He ran his hand around my stomach. "We should name her Elizabeth, call her Lizzy…"

I tilted my head back and narrowed my gaze on him. "We are not naming our daughter Elizabeth Bennett."

He grinned at me. "Jane? Lydia? Kitty?"

A laugh left me. "How do you know all those names?"

"My mother was obsessed. She used to hog the TV when my dad wasn't around and watch Colin Firth emerge from the water over and over and over again." He shook his head.

Couldn't knock his mom for that. "Well, yeah, it's Colin Firth."

He quirked a brow at me. "Do I need to go jump in that pool and emerge from the water to knock that man from your mind?"

I shrugged. "It wouldn't hurt." A sigh left me as I looked out on what would be ours.

Richard's phone chimed and he woke it up, a smile filling his face as he read the text.

"What?"

"They accepted." He leaned down and pressed his lips to mine. "We have a house."

"We have a house? This house?" Tears filled my eyes again.

"It's okay, baby," he cooed as he pulled me closer.

We had a house. A house our little girl would be born into. One with a pool to play in, and a yard to run around in.

I believed in him, in us, even when he failed me, even when I pushed him away. Because I loved him in a way I'd never loved anyone. He had my whole heart, and I finally knew I had his.

We could start over as a unit. Together. United.

A family.

And it all started with that night.

EPILOGUE

One year later...

THE LAST YEAR HADN'T BEEN AS PICTURE PERFECT AS I'D hoped, but that didn't mean we weren't happy, and that I wasn't still hopelessly in love with Richard. His insecurities ran deep, but he worked hard to give me the chance…to give us the chance to succeed where he hadn't with Desiree. And he made sure every single day to show me he loved me.

Thanks to Keenan's glowing endorsements to many of his ex-teammates and friends, along with Wyatt spreading the word, Bennett Sports Advisors grew by leaps and bounds. Within six months he had fifteen employees, and after a year he doubled that. He needed all the help as they had grown to over two hundred clients—a number that continued to increase weekly thanks to word of mouth.

"Finally," I said as the dryer went off.

It'd been over a year since Richard bought the brown teddy bear I was pulling out of the dryer, but it was our daughter's favorite snuggle toy, which she'd spit up on.

I walked back to the porch, grabbing a glass of water in the kitchen on my way. Richard sat in one of the chairs, his ever watchful eye on our daughter while he talked on the phone with a client.

Cassandra Anne Bennett was born happy and healthy a week

before her due date, and from that moment she was the ruler of our home.

"What's this?" I asked, my expression going wide with exaggerated surprise. Cassandra's chubby face lit up as her uncoordinated, but strong, finger and thumb reached out to take the teddy bear from me.

Her feet kicked in excitement, and she did a little grunt of happiness before babbling "mamamama" over and over.

"Look, I know you want a new Bentley, but do you *need* one? That money can be invested in a business and in a year you'll have your money back and can buy the car with the profits…mm-hmm…I get that, but what happens if you get a career-ending injury? No, I'm not trying to put that on you, I'm just saying you need to invest in your future outside of football."

He stood and began pacing. I watched as he tried to talk sense into another newly signed athlete, smiling when he did a fist pump. That always meant he'd gotten through to them.

Other players he'd helped in the past moved their business to him, and right before Cassandra was born, he had a growing income again. Which was good, and settled his anxiety about the financial investment of opening his own business. It also helped that his condo sold shortly after we moved into our dream home.

"Okay, I'll have Chad get you a list of potential investments for you to go over by this afternoon. Thank you for trusting me, Jaden. Good talking to you."

He turned to me and smiled.

"Good job, baby."

He leaned down and pressed his lips to mine on his way down to the floor.

"Dadada," Cassandra said, turning toward her daddy and crawling closer.

"Hello, my sweet pea." He picked her up and sat her on his lap. "Is Teddy all clean now?"

She blew bubbles, having no clue what he was saying to her, but she always intently paid attention to his voice.

"She is growing so much," I said with a small pout.

"Baby number two, Mrs. Bennett. I'm ready."

I smiled and shook my head at his ridiculousness, then looked down to the rings on my finger. It still was hard to believe a year ago we were broken up. So much had changed, including my last name.

At Christmas we'd had a small ceremony with family and a few close friends at my parents' house. Richard's parents came, and though civil, I understood his reluctance about my meeting them.

Most of his father's comments were minor, but when he said something about how we shouldn't have had a bastard child, I lost it. After I was done going off on him, he simply gave a nod and said, "She's a keeper," and headed to the bar.

His mother was completely smitten by Cassandra and pretty much refused to let anyone else hold her. Part of me wondered if she wasn't going to sneak off with our baby, but I realized she was simply trying to get as much time in with her first grandchild as she could, because there was no telling when she would see her again.

That was when I made a change and we started having weekly video chats with them. At the same time, it began to mend Richard's relationship with his parents.

Susie even came out from California with her partner, and they stayed to spend Christmas with us.

"Do we have everything we need for Saturday?" he asked.

I nodded. It was our first time hosting anything at the house, and we'd spent the last few weeks getting the house cleaned and a menu created.

For the Fourth of July, we had decided to invite everyone over for a pool party. It was a combination celebration for the holiday and the housewarming party we never threw.

"Anybody here?" Jenna called out.

"On the porch!" I called back.

Jenna appeared in the doorway with plastic bags filled with chips. She held them out. "My contribution to food."

"I thought you were bringing Ichigo Ame?" Just the mention of the candied strawberries had my mouth salivating.

Her eyes narrowed on me. "And what has the last week been?"

"Hell?"

She nodded. "There's just no time."

I gave her the biggest pout I could.

"Oh, come on! I'm exhausted."

"She's bringing out the guilt, I see," Brent said with a chuckle from behind Jenna. There were more bags in his hand, and I wondered what all they'd brought.

Shortly before Cassandra was born, Jenna's lease was up and she did indeed move in with Brent. It sucked that we were now fifteen minutes away from each other, but we still got to see each other every day at the office.

They went back to the gala for New Year's Eve where Brent proposed. Being a bride was never high up on Jenna's priority list, so it didn't surprise me when she came to me and told me they were getting married at the courthouse and wanted us there as witnesses. Jenna Okada became Jenna Young on February first.

"What do you have to be so exhausted for?" I asked, teasing her.

She bit down on her lower lip and glanced toward Brent.

"What is that?" I asked, my sixth sense perking up.

"What?"

I narrowed my gaze on her. "That conspiratorial look. I know that look." She couldn't hide from me.

"I told you she'd know something was wrong," Jenna said, jabbing Brent in the stomach with her elbow.

"I think you're just so excited to tell her," he said with a chuckle.

"Tell me what?"

Jenna beamed at me. "Remember how you said long ago that one time was all it took?"

My jaw dropped open, and I stared at her in frozen shock

before a screech left me and I jumped up to wrap my arms around her.

"Oh my God!" We both giggled and squealed, much to the entertainment of the men around us. Even Cassie piped in with her own little squeal, wanting to join in the fun.

"I'm missing something," Richard said with a sigh behind me. "I'm always missing something."

"Jenna's pregnant!" I cried out. "When are you due?"

"We just found out yesterday that baby Young is coming on Valentine's Day."

I glanced over at Richard. "You hear that, baby? Valentine's Day."

He nodded and smiled.

Jenna's gaze bounced between us. "Oh, now what are you two being sneaky about?"

"We're going to have to start a betting pool," Richard said, grinning at Brent.

"What are we betting on?" Brent asked.

"Which of our wives is going to give birth first."

Jenna's mouth popped open. "No way! The same day?"

"Technically the twelfth."

"We're going to be pregnant together!" Jenna squealed and threw her arms around me.

I loved that once again I wouldn't be going through it again on my own. Being pregnant with Hannah had been such a help to me, especially in the difficult times.

"Richard, you dog," Jenna said with a smirk.

He chuckled at her and shook his head. "I told her the next one was a boy. I was right about Cassie. I'm going to be right about this one, too."

"It's a girl," I whispered.

Richard wrapped his arms around my waist and pressed his lips to my temple. "Boy."

I loved my husband. I loved my daughter. I loved my friends.

Most of all, I loved my life.

I had never imagined how one night could change everything, but it had. In the most spectacular way, love struck. Ignited and burned more brightly than the hottest sun. It brought us together, tied us to one another.

One spilled drink.

One glance.

One magical night.

The End

AFTER ALL THE WORDS AND ALL THE THINGS...

When I began working on my piece for the Wild in the Windy City Anthology I was struggling. I wasn't connecting to ideas, and while talking to a friend she said to me "Why don't you do an office romance? You love those."

And she was right. I do love those.

I immediately connected to this idea and a story blossomed and a connection so powerful that I knew it had to continue past that night.

I hope you enjoyed Richard and Natasha's story. If by chance it wasn't for you, I hope you will still give me a chance to become one of your favorite authors.

ABOUT THE AUTHOR

K.I. Lynn is the *USA Today* Bestselling Author from The Bend Anthology and the Amazon Bestsellers, *Breach* and *Becoming Mrs Lockwood*. She spent her life in the arts, everything from music to painting and ceramics, then to writing. Characters have always run around in her head, acting out their stories, but it wasn't until later in life she would put them to pen. It would turn out to be the one thing she was really passionate about.

Since she began posting stories online, she's garnered acclaim for her diverse stories and hard hitting writing style. Two stories and characters are never the same, her brain moving through different ideas faster than she can write them down as it also plots its quest for world domination…or cheese. Whichever is easier to obtain… Usually it's cheese.

Website—www.kilynnauthor.com
Facebook—https://www.facebook.com/kilynn.breach
Twitter—twitter.com/KI_Lynn_
Instagram—www.instagram.com/k.i.lynn
Get my Newsletter—http://bit.ly/1U9NSoC

MORE BOOKS FROM K.I. LYNN!

That Night

I got pregnant on New Year's Eve.
That night was hands down the best night of my life. A magical night with the man of my dreams.

The aftermath changed everything.

After weeks of silence from him and a positive pregnancy test, it was safe to say I was in full out panic mode.

Until I walked into a conference room only to find Mr. Man-of-my-dreams-father-of-my-unborn-child at the head of the table.

Turns out the VP of finance isn't an old boring guy with white hair.

Two different cities.

A baby on the way.

An intense attraction.

And he's technically my boss.

Life just got even more complicated.

Find out more here—**books2read.com/ThatNightKILynn**

Abducted

The mafia never lets you go.

I thought I was safe, free, but I never expected to find myself locked in a cage.

I'm in his territory. His prison.

The beast.

A fate worse than death awaits me if I can't get away, so when the opportunity of salvation presents itself I grab it, even if I'm unsure if I can trust the hand I'm holding.

The only way out is through, exposing secrets and spilling blood.

Things aren't how they appear. Nobody is what they seem.

Not even me.

Find out more here—**books2read.com/AbductedKILynn**

Forever and All The Afters

He promised me forever.

Then he boarded a plane for a college a thousand miles away and never returned. A decade later there's a ring on my finger with a new promise from a new love.

Just as my life falls into place, pretty as the pages of a magazine, my world is knocked over. The moment he touches me everything around me begins to crack, exposing all the lies I've told myself.

Every glance reminds me. Every touch ignites.

Things aren't how they used to be.

Love isn't easy.

Find out more here—books2read.com/ForeverAndAllTheAfters

Welcome to the Cameo Hotel

I get what I want.

When I walked through the door of the Cameo Hotel I didn't expect such a beauty to be working the front desk.

The effect she has on me is intense, and I make her life a living hell because of it.

I love her spirit, her internal defiance when completing the most inane task I assign her. My two week stay has turned into unending, just to be near her.

She's under my every command if she wants to keep me happy.

There's one last thing I want.

Her.

Find out more here—
books2read.com/WelcomeToTheCameoHotel

Becoming Mrs. Lockwood

Every girl has dreams of meeting Prince Charming, or at least I know I did.

A fairy tale-like meeting of love at first site.

Real life and fairy tales are very different.

I'm just a small town Indiana girl that had a chance encounter with one of Hollywood's golden boys. You may think you know where this story goes—not even close.

Life is different. Marriage is hard. It's even worse when you're strangers.

Find out more here—
books2read.com/BecomingMrsLockwood

Six

I had a one-night stand. It wasn't my first, but it would be my last.

A gun to the head.

A trained killer.

A deadly conspiracy.

Kidnapped and on the run, my life and death is in the hands of a sadist captor who happens to be my one-night stand. Armed with countless weapons, money, and new identities, the man I call Six drags me around the world.

The manhunt is on and Six is the next target. Can we find out who is killing off the Cleaners before they find us?

Two down, seven to go.

When it's all over he'll finish the job that dropped him into my life, and end it.

Stockholm Syndrome meets bucket list, and the question of what would you do to live before you died. The questions aren't always answered in black and white. Gray becomes the norm as my morals are tested.

Death is a tragedy, and I'll do anything to stay alive.

Are you ready for the last ride of your life? Six has a gun to your head—what would you do?

This isn't a love story.

It's a death story.

Find out more here—
books2read.com/Six-KILynn
Check out the Trailer—youtu.be/fzpON3PadIA

Breach Book 1

His body was sin, his cock was sin, and I was a sinner.

To keep myself safe I hide in the world and let life move around me.

My new partner, Nathan, isn't safe. Far from it.

The darkness coils around him, hidden by a shield created by a blinding smile. But those who live in shadows see past the façade we create.

Even in darkness, there is light. A spark that ignites, then explodes.

Every filthy word from his mouth, every possessive touch—I crave them, need them. Violent and passionate and everything I need to fill the void inside me, but one thing is missing.

He can never love me.

More than my heart is on the line, and I don't know if I'll survive our breach.

Find out more here—
books2read.com/Breach

The Executive

Business is king, and I have an empire to topple.

Ivy is my new assistant and a threat to me. She's my undoing. If ever I was to believe in a cosmic connection, it was the moment I met her.

For years I've had one goal--revenge. As CEO, I have crafted a strategic plan for business, but never a life beyond.

With one touch from her, the veil is lifted. Things are different, and every moment I'm near her, my world begins to change.

A wall of propriety keeps me from her. I need her as my pawn in this war, beside me in battle. Sharing the secrets of my enemies, and her desires in my bed. Her body to claim as mine.

Getting what I want has consequences.

Collateral damage is real.

In the game of crushing kings of men, I never planned on my heart being a sacrifice.

Find out more here –
books2read.com/TheExecutive

Cocksure
Co-written with Olivia Kelley
A life altering lie, ten years, and one wild night later, the game has changed.

Niko

My life is great. I love my job, have awesome friends, and a great family.

Women love me, even if they know it's just for a night.

I always thought love at first sight was bullshit. Then she came storming into my life. She tore through my every rule, rocked my world, and knocked me on my ass.

There's only one problem…she lied.+

Turns out my best friend's little sister isn't so little anymore.

Everly

I stole a night with my fantasy. Lied to him.

After ten years of not seeing each other, Niko doesn't even recognize me.

So I take what I want from him, what I need from him. Without worry. Without consequence.

What I didn't count on was the lingering need for him.

Once the truth is out, the game changes. There are consequences.

I should have known nothing in my life is ever simple.

My brother is going to kill his best friend and I have nine months to figure out what I want.

Find out more here—
books2read.com/Cocksure-Lynn-Kelley

Need Book 1
Co-written with N. Isabelle Blanco

I was Kira's from the first moment I saw her. Maybe it was love at first sight, but I was only ten.

She became my best friend.

My crush.

The girl I can't live without.

But I have to.

She was almost mine, but my father took away my chance.

Now she lives across the hall from me. Instead of the title of girlfriend, she's now my stepsister.

But that doesn't stop how I feel, how I want her. Thankfully, I'm off to college two hundred miles away, but even that doesn't help.

She's under my skin, all around me, and I watch her morph from a sexy teenager to an irresistible woman.

I can't take it anymore, I need her.

Is it possible to ever be happy without the one person you *need*?

"I'm Brayden, baby. The man you've been dreaming about your whole life. And I'm about to fucking show you why."

Part 1 of a 3 part series.

Find out more here—
books2read.com/NeedSeries

CPSIA information can be obtained
at www.ICGtesting.com
Printed in the USA
FSHW012220190420
69366FS